IT'S NOW OR NEVER

IT'S NOW OR NEVER

Cameron Ventura

Hidden Shelf Publishing House
P.O. Box 4168, McCall, ID 83638
www.hiddenshelfbooks.com

Cover art: Cameron Ventura

Graphic design: Allison Kaukola

Interior layout: Sarah Harris

Library of Congress Cataloguing-in-Publication Data

Ventura, Cameron
It's Now or Never

ISBN: 0999646625
ISBN-13: 978-0-9996466-2-5

Printed in the United States of America

Table of Contents

MAP OF MAGPIE MINE

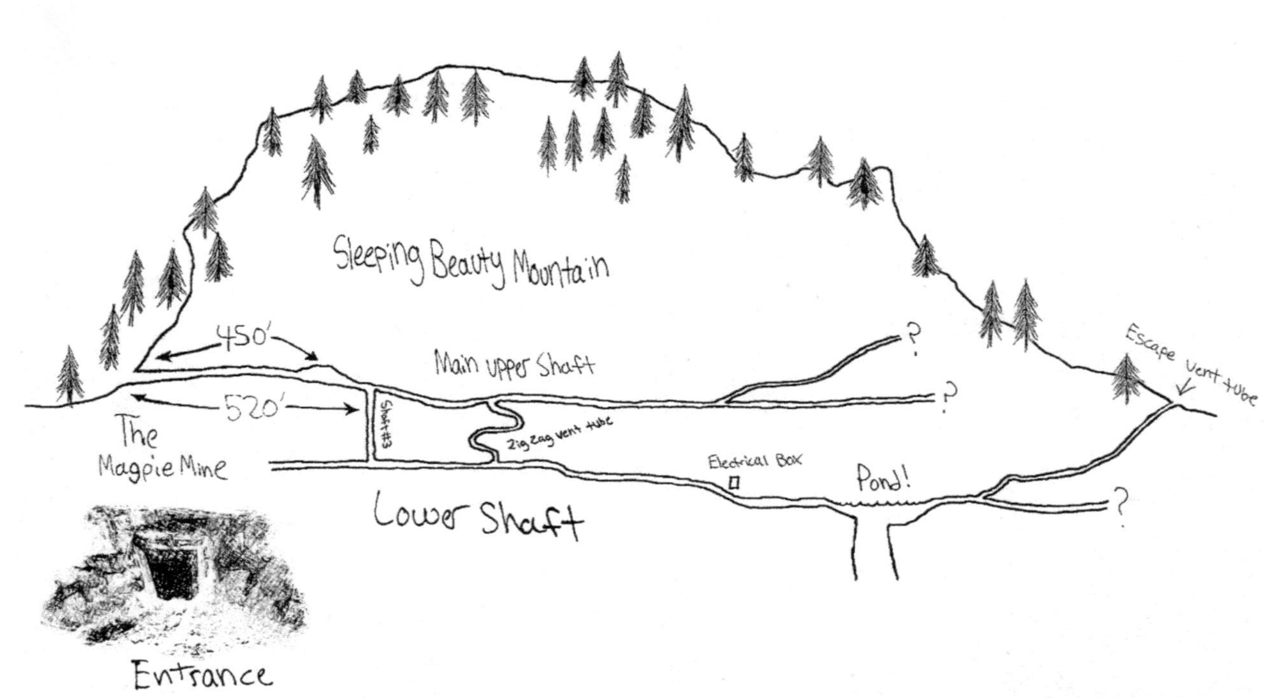

Chapter 1

DOWN A DEEP, DARK SHAFT

Stars filled my vision. A million mini-fireworks were exploding in front of my face. Only it was pitch black.

I'd been moving slowly, hand-over-hand along a rusty cable when one of them gave way and suddenly sagged. Then I was swinging through space, the lights went out, and I crashed into the wall.

As for the stars, I'd learned a long time ago that my eyes never liked total darkness; they always filled the black curtain of my sight with colorful sparkles.

"Oh man," James said in a grouchy voice. I heard him but my mind was all fuzzy. "You okay?"

I didn't say anything for a few seconds. My head hurt and my hands were screaming pain as I gripped the cables.

"Cal, are you there?"

"Yeah, where's your light?" I asked.

"Down at the bottom," he said. "I saw you swinging and dropped it. Where's yours?"

"In my pocket. But I'm hanging here." I kicked off from the wall and frantically started to swing myself to find anything to stand on. One foot found something.

"I'm . . . I'm on a beam," I whispered.

"Well, get yer light out," James ordered in a loud whisper. I fumbled around, got it out, and clicked it on. I could see his light shattered on the rock floor of the lower mine shaft. He was looking down too.

"Well, that's toast," he grumbled. "Aim yer light on the platform and I'll get the rest of the way down."

He looked up at me. "Yer bleeding," he whispered. I wiped my hand across my forehead and sure enough, I was leaking blood. "Here, throw me your light so you have both hands," he suggested.

"If you miss, we're . . ." I said.

"I know. I'm not going to drop it," he said. "Now come on! We don't got all day here!"

He was right. In fact, we didn't have much time at all, so I gently tossed my light down to him, which he caught. Now that I had both hands, I started down the shaft again. James quickly navigated around until he could jump down the six or so feet to the rickety platform. It wobbled and I thought for sure it was going to collapse, but it held. The tall ladder that stuck up through the hatch and dropped the last ten feet or so was missing a bunch of rungs so James had to get creative to reach the floor of Shaft #3. I was still about halfway through the tangle of junk, and needed to get down . . . and fast.

* * *

We'd stumbled across the vertical shaft that morning and decided to explore. We named it Shaft #3. At first, after we found it, James had held a cable and leaned out and aimed his light down into the blackness. I instantly got the heebie-jeebies and wobbled back a few steps. Heights will always pull the plug and drain the juice out of me. I couldn't even see what he was looking at . . . and I kind of didn't want to.

"Hold on, Cal," James said, "there's no water down there." He'd scrambled out onto a huge beam that spanned the top of the gaping hole. "Wow, it's deep," he added and looked at me with his let's-check-it-out grin. I inched back to the lip of the shaft and peered over the edge.

"Come out on this beam so you can see better," he prodded.

I sat down on the edge and scooted closer to the beam. "Doesn't look sturdy," I said.

"It'll hold," James said and slapped the rough wood. "Look at this thing . . . it's massive. It's holding me, isn't it?"

I put my hands on it, looked down, and seized up.

James was waving his light around, catching the tangle of beams, pipes, cables, and wires that crisscrossed the huge square hole in the floor. It was probably close to a hundred feet deep. James' light barely touched the floor. It was drippy and damp, but at least not full of water.

"James . . ."

"What?"

I didn't finish. I didn't know what to say.

"I wonder what's down there?" he asked, more to himself than me.

We'd discovered the Magpie mine a few months ago and had barely started to explore it. Mainly because it was so far back in the hills behind Mud Lake, Washington, the little town where we lived. It took us around three hours to ride our bikes that far, so we'd only been there a few times.

Nevertheless, we considered it ours because we could tell no one had been there in years. The tiny two-track road was overgrown and there hadn't been any footprints. There were some animal tracks going in and out of the mine, which had us a little concerned. Every time we'd ride up from Mud Lake, we tried to bring some things that we could leave—flashlight batteries, peanut butter and jelly, a couple of blankets. Rope, though, hadn't made it up yet.

* * *

Sorry, climbing down into the deep darkness of Shaft #3 did not at all look safe.

"I think we need some rope and stuff before we . . ."

James interrupted me. "Cal, come on. If we stopped what we were doing to go get ropes 'n stuff every time we discovered something interesting, we'd never do anything."

I just looked down the hole and frowned. Shaft #3 connected the upper shaft to a lower one, and hadn't been used in probably fifty years. Now, all that stuff had collapsed into itself and was pretty much a giant game of pick up sticks.

"I'm checkin' this out," James finally said. "You can stay here and watch if you want, but I'm goin' down." And he jumped down to a lower beam and held onto some wires, just in case it gave way. "It's holding," he said.

I could feel myself starting to breathe in and out the way I do when I get nervous. It happens all the time when James jumps into something and I need to think it through. The trouble is, he doesn't want to think things through, he wants to charge ahead, which leaves me sitting back and watching for a while.

He always makes everything look so easy that I usually decide to jump in too. And that's where we're different. James is coordinated and moves like a monkey in the trees; I move slow and deliberate.

I watched as James jumped, landed on another beam, caught his balance and then crab-walked across it. He grabbed a bundle of cables and swung over to another large beam and looked up at me.

"It's easy," he said. I just nodded and started to follow his lead.

If James was Tarzan, swinging through the jungle, I was more like a sloth I'd seen on Wild Kingdom.

James patiently waited for me while aiming his flashlight, pointing out my next handhold, and where I should put my feet. The trouble was he kept hitting my face with the light.

"Yer doin' good," he said.

"Well, you're blinding me," I said back. The truth is that I was freaking out. I was turning into rubber and losing my strength because of my nerves. Literally, I was slowly slithering down through a mishmash of junk.

I was making progress, thanks to James' tips and pointers. Then I found myself at a wall of bolts.

"Okay, Spiderman. Yer gonna just climb down the bolts," James said.

Just climb down the bolts, I thought. Just like Spiderman. I glanced down—not a good idea for me. I started panting again, and then got dizzy from the heavy breathing.

"Don't look down, Cal. Just do it."

"Sorry," I muttered and held on to one giant bolt and stepped down to the next one. I was worried I was going to pass out. "Spiderman doesn't get Jello legs," I said out loud.

"You don't know that," James laughed. "Maybe the first few times he swung across those buildings he did."

"Maybe," I agreed.

I finally ran out of bolts and reached a cross beam that made sort of a ledge. I had to just rest and let my legs relax.

"Jello legs," I muttered and he laughed.

"Okay, hand-over-hand along the cables," he instructed, and waggled his light along the thick steel ropes. "It's easy."

"For you . . . I know how to hand-over-hand . . . quit bugging me," I snapped.

"Gawl, what a crab," he snickered.

I sucked in a breath and started across. I wanted to go fast. I wanted to do it in four swings, but I was crawling forward. Suddenly, I heard something and froze . . . hanging there in the middle of the gaping hole.

"What?" he asked.

"Shush," I whispered. "Listen!"

A laugh traveled through the mine's tunnels and reached

us in the shaft. It sounded miles away or under a blanket. I listened hard to hear if we'd actually heard someone through the twists and curves of the old mine.

"Someone's coming," James said in a soft voice.

"Could be someone from the old mining company," I said. "We'd be in a bunch a trouble if they found us."

"Who cares about that," James said. "We just don't want 'em sealing it up. So get a move on."

A spooky wolf howl was followed by another laugh. It was an older voice. Kids whoop or giggle, and that wasn't a kid's voice. Then I heard a second voice. Two older guys, I thought. I was suddenly relieved that we'd hidden our bikes so they didn't know we were in here. Whoever it was didn't seem to care if anyone heard them.

Me and James know that talking loud or shouting in a mine is a terrible idea. The sound's vibrations can cause things to come crashing down. Their loud laughs said these guys didn't care much about that. They were getting closer and I had to get myself going again.

"Come on, Cal," James whispered as loud as he dared. He quit watching me and went back to working his way down.

I grabbed the bundle of cables and started to hand-over-hand. Suddenly they jerked and dropped a foot or so. James looked up.

"What happened?"

I didn't answer . . . just sped up.

James waggled his light again to get me going. That's when the cable let loose and I swung and smashed into the stone wall. And that's when James dropped his flashlight and we were in total darkness.

* * *

The voices were getting close enough that we could kind of make out words. I started to scramble—not one of my skills. Math, maps, figuring out why something's a bad idea . . . those are my best abilities. Scrambling around on rusted pipes and rotten beams is almost a guarantee for trouble.

Using his monkey skills, James got down the ladder and pointed the light where I should go next. Some of the times they were good ideas, other times I just fell and rolled and grabbed whatever was close. In no time I was full of slivers from the beams and scraped up from my clumsy landings.

The voices were getting closer. Sometimes laughing and then howling to hear their echoes. I froze.

"Cal, you're so close."

James pointed to the left of the landing. "Watch that side. It's rotten."

I had to drop about six feet to reach the next beam and started to panic.

"I'm gonna climb back up there and shove you off, if you don't get a move on," he said. I looked at him, then the landing, and jumped. I made a loud *whomp* sound when I hit the dusty, crumbling wood. I saw what James meant—the left side was worm-eaten and rotten. Then I froze again.

The voices had reached where Shaft #3 meets the main shaft.

One of them said, "What's down there?"

"Dunno." Then a faint flashlight beam started bouncing off the ceiling and walls. I looked at James and he gave me another get-moving look.

I grabbed the top of the ladder and dropped down the hole as James clicked off our light and disappeared somewhere. I was left standing on the ladder, just under the platform when the voices reached the lip of the shaft. I quietly moved around the ladder so I was under the platform, and kept my face looking down.

"Just a big ol' hole," one of them said. Their flashlight lit up the shaft and flicked around off all the beams and junk that crisscrossed the shaft. When it hit the floor, it stopped for a second on James' smashed flashlight and then moved on. I suddenly saw James in the shadows from the faint glow of their light. His eyes were big and he was looking at me.

My heart was a bass drum pounding in my chest and I thought I was going to pop from holding my breath.

"Ain't goin' down that," one of the voices said.

"Not luggin' this down that hole," the other agreed.

"Come on, we're goin' my way," the first one said. He sounded gruff, almost mad. They left and we stayed still for a couple more minutes, until we heard them again, further into the main shaft.

James rushed out and helped me down the lousy ladder. I collapsed in a pile and sat panting for a few seconds. I looked up at him.

"Thanks," was all I could say.

"Come on," he said, sounding suddenly anxious. He grabbed me and helped me out of sight.

"What's the matter? They're gone," I said.

"Maybe. I hope so. That was Derrick Carter," he whispered.

"Who's Derrick Carter?" I asked in the smallest whisper I had.

"No one we want to meet down here," he answered.

I've never really seen James scared, but whoever Derrick Carter was had him worried. He kept glancing up to the top of the shaft. I did too, expecting them to come back.

"Let's get out of sight," he said. He walked and I crawled into the shadows.

"I think we need to find a way out down this way," he said and pointed down the tunnel.

"Let's just climb back up," I suggested. He shook his

head.

"Na-ah, not gettin' caught up there by Derrick Carter." He took the light and walked down the tunnel a little ways. I just sat and watched. I could tell there was no other option but down the tunnel, and he was impatient.

"It's mostly dry," he whispered. He didn't wait for any of my objections or scientific analyzing; he just started walking. So, I wobbled along behind him.

The blackness that surrounded us was thick. The yellow beam of my wimpy little army flashlight tried to push back the gloom, but it didn't have a chance. We could only see about twenty or thirty feet and then the light was swallowed up and gone. I kept glancing back behind us, which was stupid; all that was back there was the darkness we'd just passed through. I was one constant shudder—some from the chilled air that was hitting us in the face, and some from the ghosts that I figured were staying out of sight, but right on our heels.

"Who's Derrick Carter?" I asked after we'd walked a while.

"Went to Mud Lake when I was in elementary. In some kind a trouble about every day." He thought for a little while, then added, "The Carters are a nest of oddballs who live way out of town. Derrick dropped out of high school a few years ago. Most everyone knows he's the meanest kid around."

My imagination started working overtime because we were suddenly in a mine shaft—with someone named Derrick Carter—who James just said was the meanest kid he'd ever met. It was bad enough wondering what sort of slimy *thing* might be following us down in the depths of the Magpie mine; having Derrick Carter nosing around somewhere above our heads was almost more than I could take. I shook like someone had just electrocuted me.

"What's he doing up here?" I asked, knowing James was wondering the same thing.

"Dunno . . . something he shouldn't, I'll bet."

Right then, we saw a small tunnel that joined the main one we were in.

"Here we go," James said in a soft voice.

As we approached, James started to swing the light to have a look when we heard them again. Derrick and his pal were coming down the tunnel. James jammed the light into his shirt and we dashed off deeper down into the tunnel, trying our best to be quiet. That's not easy when you're tripping and stumbling over rocks and junk that litters old mines.

We rounded a corner and stopped to catch our breath. Derrick and his friend must have reached the main shaft because we heard a loud laugh and then some talking.

Whoever was doing all the laughing sure had an overactive funny bone. Or the other one told great jokes.

My gramps was a jokester and could get me laughing so hard I'd have to leave the table. Gram always gave him a look, but she loved seeing me get so silly. These guys though, I didn't think they were the joke-telling type. One sounded mean and scary. The other voice sounded kind of dumb or slow.

Once they reached the lower shaft, we started to move faster. There were a few turns where we stopped to listen. They were still coming, so we kept going deeper and deeper into the mine.

As bad as we wanted to not meet Derrick Carter down in the Magpie mine, the last turn we rounded stopped us dead in our tracks.

Chapter 2

MONSTERS OF THE MAGPIE

Sooner or later a person exploring a mine is going to find water, and we found ours. We stood there for a second and stared at perfectly still water, completely filling the shaft. We were trapped.

"Great," I murmured. "Water."

James hurried back to the bend and listened. We could hear them, way back. We'd been hurrying while they were just strolling along. James came back to the edge of the pool and pointed the light into the water. Then he aimed it at the walls and around the narrow cavern.

"I think there's a bend down there," he said and moved the light to indicate that the water rounded a corner. I could just make out what he was seeing. Yes, the water disappeared around a bend in the tunnel. Then James tossed a small stone out twenty feet. It made a *kerplunk*.

"Deep," he whispered.

"We could swim around that bend in the tunnel and wait," he whispered. I suddenly looked at him as a shiver ran up my back.

"You can. I'm not getting in there." I took a step back, worried something was going to crawl out and grab my leg. "I think I'll just take my chances with Derrick."

"It's just water, Cal. If there was ever a monster in there, it died of starvation." He said this in his *you sure can be a chicken* voice.

James actually took any opportunity to rib me about my fear of deep water and monsters. Right now, the prospect of a dead monster floating under the surface didn't help at all.

I let out a gasp. I'd been holding my breath.

* * *

Seriously, it takes every ounce of bravery that I have to get me into unknown water . . . particularly where I can't see the bottom. I instantly picture big slimy creatures lying around just waiting for something to nab and eat . . . ugghh. I seize up and my circuits short out.

It started when I was around six years old and my dad took me fishing for carp in shallow water down on the Columbia. Really, he was doing the fishing, I was just wading around and looking at stuff. Out of nowhere, a huge fat carp bumped into my leg and then suddenly there were hundreds of them thrashing around me. I'm sure they were big. Carp can grow to over two hundred pounds, so to a little kid, they were whales. I literally jumped out of that murky water and was done for the day . . . maybe a lifetime. Later, to add to my imagination, in my *National Geographics*, I'd seen how fat African crocodiles lay under the muddy surface of rivers and then grab wildebeests and drag them in and drown them. And then there's the stories about the Amazon Piranha. I skipped past that article four times before finally reading about what they can do to a dead cow carcass.

* * *

"I'm going back," I whispered, turning away from the black water. James followed and grabbed me.

"Cal, there's nowhere to hide," he said in a very low voice. "Derrick once killed someone's dog because it was barking too much. He'd corner kids after school and beat the living daylights out of them, and then threaten them if they ever told who did it. He stole a teacher's car when he was twelve, and drove it all the way to White Salmon."

I realized that I was stuck between Derrick Carter and the monster that maybe lived in the mine pond. I looked back at the black water.

We heard them getting closer. "He's no one we want to meet down here," James said again. He tugged on my shirt to pull me back to the pond, and I gave in. Besides, we only had the one light. And, I'd be left alone in the dark with the pond monsters.

James didn't hesitate, he just waded in. I stood at the pond's edge, frozen and shaking from the cold and the scary movies blasting in my brain.

He inched further and further out and deeper and deeper until the water reached his thigh. He looked back at me. It was the look I'd seen a hundred times, when he wants to go and I want to think it over. He threw up his arms in his *come on, Cal* gesture.

Those stories about the neighbor's dog and what Derrick did to kids after school got me moving. Also, James had my flashlight.

I shuddered, punched my leg in frustration, and waded in. I wasn't even up to my knees and I was ready to start swimming. But, James was still feeling his way with his feet and then stepping. He was shining the flashlight down into the water, trying to see the bottom. Its crazy reflection danced around on the walls and ceiling, which didn't help the already terrifying situation. I couldn't see the bottom and had to use only what I felt, so I was moving even slower. For some reason I thought the bottom would just fall away, but it seemed to slowly slope, and boy, was that water cold. It made the backs of my knees ache.

James was about twenty feet out in front of me and the water was at his belt. "I think this is as deep as it gets," he whispered, and kept inching along.

"Wait," I said in a low voice. I pointed to my ears. I'd heard a loud clatter of stuff hitting the ground. "I think they've stopped."

I turned and moved quickly out of the water and back to the corner in the shaft to listen. I heard them talking and more clatter and clunking. It was tools alright. I quietly ran back into the water toward James. "They've stopped and I heard tools." He'd stopped and was looking at me. It suddenly struck me that he was deeper than he was a few seconds ago. The water was across his stomach. He was trying to raise his feet to walk, but they seemed stuck. The movement was causing him to sink. He looked annoyed.

"I'm kinda stuck," he whispered.

"Well, hold still. It might be quicksand or a sinkhole." I'd seen quicksand on *Wild Kingdom* . . . tricky stuff.

"When you move your feet up and down," I said, "it makes you sink, so stop moving and wait." He hadn't heard me, or wasn't listening. He kept trying to lift his legs from the muck that was gripping them. He kind of lost his balance and sloshed to one side. "Don't move," I snapped again. He finally stopped and looked at me.

"We need a rope," he whispered.

"Well, we don't have one. Throw me the light and I'll find something."

I never ordered anyone to do anything, so giving one to James told him he might be in trouble. I barely caught the flashlight, once again left the water, and quickly started looking around for anything. I spied a bundle of wires following the roof of the tunnel.

"Those wires," I suggested, pointing to the ceiling.

I started to follow them up the main shaft to find where

they started, leaving him in complete darkness.

"Hey," he tried to shout and still whisper. I had to ignore him. We only had one light, and I needed it. I followed the wires for fifty feet or so, but they didn't end and there was no way for me to cut them. I couldn't even reach them. I knew I was heading right back toward Derrick and his friend. I figured there were still a couple bends in the shaft before I reached them, and I didn't see their light yet, so I kept hurrying forward. At some point, just to be safe, I tucked my flashlight under my shirt. I could barely see anything and had to really look to see if the wires were still there. Also, the clock was ticking in my head for James. In that first minute or so it took me to hurry back to the corner and listen, James had sunk into the muck a good foot, I thought. I glanced at my watch.

"Five minutes," I whispered out loud. "If he'll hold still, I can maybe make it."

I rounded a corner and the wires ended at a huge electrical box. I also saw Derrick's lights dancing on the wall just around the next bend. They were digging for something. So their shovels made that clang, swish sound of digging in rocky sand. I was hoping they wouldn't hear me. It was risky, but I had to do it. James was slowly sinking.

I aimed my light back down the shaft and looked at the box. It was at least three feet tall and rusty. It wasn't locked, so I pulled on the door. Right off it complained with a rusty squawk and I stopped. Their digging continued, so I pulled it a little more and it groaned. I stopped again. Swish, swish, clunk, swish, clunk, clang . . . they couldn't hear me. I aimed my light inside and noticed that the wires I'd been following snaked inside and bolted to giant connectors.

Great, I thought. How'm I going to get those off?

I gave the door one last little tug and it gave me a few more inches without too much noise. I reached in and started trying to bend one of the wires back and forth. It was a very thick copper wire with cloth insulation. The more I bent it back and forth, the insulation weakened and finally cracked off. Then the digging stopped. I snapped off my flashlight.

"What?" Derrick said.

"I'm hungry," the other guy whined.

"Eat rocks, stupid. I didn't bring anything."

"I want something to eat or I can't dig no more, Dee." I heard a low thud and then someone cried out in pain.

"You want me ta cook up some dirt?" Derrick hollered. I suddenly heard sniveling from the other guy, who seemed to be crying. I guessed they weren't coming any further into the mine and their lights gave me just enough brightness to see and keep bending the wire.

"Good grief, cut out the cryin', Cletus," Derrick growled. One shovel started digging again.

I looked at my watch. I'd been gone almost five minutes. I was really getting worried that James might be under water by now.

"Come on, Cleets. Stop it with the crying, big guy," Derrick said. He was trying to sound nicer.

"Ya hit me with yer shovel, Dee," Cletus sobbed.

"I know I did," Derrick said, and chuckled. "Couldn't a hurt that much. Let's get this job done and I'll get you a burger at the cafe. Maybe even a double patty."

There was a pause. "With extra pickles?" Cletus asked.

"A bucket of 'em, dummy," Derrick said. Cletus huffed out a kind of laugh and started working again. The noise helped me work faster on the wire. It was getting hot from the friction and burned my fingers. I didn't care, I had to break it free.

Snap. It broke. I started pushing it up through the top and watched it sag down from the insulator rings so I could grab it.

"Gimme the canteen, I'm parched," Derrick ordered

from around the bend. He'd stopped digging, so I stopped messing with the wire. I was almost panicked, but I had to wait.

There was a bunch of clunking and clanking . . .

"Cletus, you're a pig," Derrick hollered. "It's almost empty!"

"I brought it. I can sip if I wanna," Cletus argued back.

"Learn ta share, ya big hog," Derrick growled.

Then a scuffle broke out. I could hear them grunting and struggling and banging into their tools. I used the noisy moment to whip the wire to get it to slide through the next insulator ring. I quickly pulled the wire through and did the same with the next ring. Then their brawl stopped and so did I.

"You play too rough, Dee," Cletus howled, sounding like he was half laughing and half meaning it.

"You think that's rough, wait'll I get serious," Derrick snarled back at him. "Now get back to work, or we'll be here all night . . . and that means you ain't gettin' any burger."

They started digging again.

"They're gonna cave this place in they're so noisy," I whispered to myself.

I was working my way back to James when I spotted a drill rod. Perfect, I thought, and used it to grab the wire and pull it through the rings.

When I got back to the pond, the water was up to James' chin. His eyes were as big as half dollars.

"What took ya so long?"

"Oh, I had a sandwich with those guys," I casually said back at him while coiling the thick wire so I could toss it.

"Derrick's not as mean as you think. Gave me his coke, and offered to come get you out."

"Oh shut up," James snapped back. He wasn't in the mood for jokes. But neither was I. Finally, the thick wire was beginning to cooperate.

"I'm kind a slow when I'm trying to be invisible," I said, wading out to almost where I'd been before while feeling the bottom with one foot out front. It was rocky, so I decided I was far enough. I wasn't keen on getting stuck too.

"Are you gonna take all day, Calvin? Throw me the wire!" He was sounding a bit panicked and had his hands up.

Calvin. I hated for James to call me "Calvin" and he knew it.

"Shut up, Ralph," I shot back. James hated his middle name.

"Just hurry up . . . I can't move my legs!"

I could still kind of hear those guys digging and arguing, so I tossed the wire. It made a little splash and I winced. They didn't hear it though. James instantly pulled and the wire tightened. I started backing up and the wire stretched tightrope tight, but James wasn't moving. In fact, I pulled him underwater. I let off and he popped back up. The swish of the water sounded really loud and I looked back up the shaft and listened. One of the guys let out a loud laugh, so I wrapped the wire around my waist, turned toward shore, and started really pulling. I leaned against James' weight and he went underwater again. I could feel my feet sinking too, so I let off and dashed to the shore and dry ground. James popped up again. He didn't look happy about being dunked.

"I was sinking," I whispered and cinched the wire around my waist again, pulling with all my strength. I leaned away from James as if I was fighting a big wind. He went under again, but I started to move, which meant so was he. Then his head and shoulders popped up. I kept pulling and dragged him to where the bottom was solid. He sloshed out and flopped down on the sandy floor. He was drenched and covered in mud. And red. Whatever was in that water had turned him red!

"Wow, quicksand," I said.

"Yeah, couldn't move a muscle. It was like cement. Yew,

tastes nasty too," he muttered and wiped his face on my shirt.

"You looked scared." I winced, instantly wishing I hadn't said that.

"I wasn't scared, Cal. Just a little of that phob stuff."

"Phob? You mean, phobia?"

"Yeah, phobia . . . classer-phob or something."

"You mean, claustrophobia."

"Yeah, just can't stand tight places too long."

James had never said he got claustrophobia before, so this was new news. Someone told me my fear of water was called hydrophobia. Up till then I'd only heard of claustrophobia.

"I knew you'd get me out, so I just held on," he said while grinning and slugging my shoulder. He spit between his legs again and wiped his face.

"What are they doing?" he asked and looked over his shoulder toward Derrick and Cletus.

"Digging."

"You mean mining kind of digging?" he asked.

"Ah, I don't no. They're digging a hole or something."

He thought about that, then said, "I wonder what they're digging?"

I didn't say anything because I didn't know. And truthfully, I didn't want to know. We just sat there while he spit and thought.

"I kinda wanna know what they're doin'," he finally said.

The wheels in James' head were turning. He got up and walked to the edge of our flashlight beam. "How far back are they?"

"Fifty yards or so."

"And you were close enough to hear them?

"Oh yeah. They were arguing about Cletus hogging all the water in the canteen."

"Cletus? The other guy's Cletus? His cousin Cletus?"

"I dunno. That's what Derrick was calling him . . . and

other things. He's sure dumb, whoever he is. Is Derrick's cousin a lunkhead?"

"Lunkhead would be giving Cletus a little too much credit," James said. "More like a dunderhead."

I had no idea what the difference was between a lunkhead and a dunderhead. I just suspected that Cletus was a few bricks short of a load. That's what Gramps used to say about people who were not quite "with the program."

"Let go see what they're doing," James suggested.

I instantly eyed him. "You said that Derrick's the meanest kid you'd ever met."

"Yeah, well, I'm not gonna reintroduce myself," he said in a smirky kind of way. "We'll hide out where you were, and . . ."

I cut him off.

"There's no hiding, James. If they walk around the corner, there's nowhere to go. It's a straight line tunnel for a hundred feet."

He thought about that. "Well, I'll go then, have a listen to see if I can discover anything, and come right back." That smile suddenly appeared. He knew I'd never, in a million years, stay here by this water and wait in the pitch black dark. And I knew that once an idea got in his head, you may as well be pulling teeth from a bear to change it. Nevertheless, I stared at him.

"Meanest kid," I reminded him.

"Yup, probably wouldn't save his mom if she was sinkin' in that mucky quicksand."

This was all said in a low whisper, of course, as we could still hear them back there digging and talking and arguing.

"Five minutes is all," I said, hoping it was a good compromise. He grinned and took the light from me and we started walking back toward the meanest kid James had ever known and his box-of-rocks cousin.

When we reached the electrical box, I tapped his shoulder to indicate where I had found the wire. We started to move forward but I grabbed his sleeve and shook my head. I also tapped my watch. He just grinned and hunkered down.

"Who comes all the way down here to dig a hole?" he whispered.

"Obviously, those two," I answered.

"Dee, I want onions on my hamburger too," Cletus said. He must dream about hamburgers, I thought. James looked at me. I whispered in his ear.

"Cletus was complaining about being hungry and Derrick said he'd buy him a hamburger when they were done." James had to bury his face into his soggy shirt to stifle a laugh.

Finally he said, "All the Carters are a bunch of knuckleheads, but that Cletus takes the cake."

They'd stopped digging and we heard a dragging sound, and then a thunk. James looked back at me and I just shrugged my shoulders.

"What was that?" James wondered.

"Treasure?" I suggested. His eyebrows went up at the thought of buried treasure. He slugged me in the shoulder. I slugged him back.

Right then Derrick said, "This is my special project, Cleets. So no tellin' my momma 'bout it. Got it?"

"Ahhh, what's I 'pose ta say, Dee?"

"*Nothin'* is what yer supposed to say. Just keep yer big fat mouth shut."

"Well, that's gonna be hard."

"Shut up, Cleets. Yer drivin' me nuts with your whinin' an' complainin', an' drinkin' all the water."

There was a long pause and then a few shovels of sand and gravel hit something wooden.

"I dunno why I brought you on this job, anyway," Derrick grumbled. "Can't trust you to be a friend, or do yer share of the work, or even keep yer mouth buttoned up."

"They'll kill us, Dee. Kill us and then . . ."

"Can't you get it through yer thick head that I can do

my own side jobs? There ain't gonna be any killin' cuz they ain't gonna know," Derrick said, starting to sound mad.

I was looking at James and gave him a little nudge and motioned to go back. The mention of someone getting killed got my attention. James shook his head, no.

"I've thought it through, Cleets," Derrick said. He then laughed. But it wasn't a funny laugh, it was a scary laugh. The shoveling stopped.

"Auntie'll be so mad if she knows," Cletus said.

"Well, she ain't hearin' nothin' from me," Derrick said in a sarcastic tone. "And she ain't gonna hear nothin' from you, neither." Now he sounded dangerous.

"I'm no good at pretending, Dee. You know that," Cletus whined.

"Well, it's pretend we didn't come up here or you're gonna be fish food if I find out you said anything."

I looked back at James and he looked at me. I mouthed "Fish food?"

There was a long silence, then their shovels started working again.

"There," Derrick said, "that's all settled down, nice and tight, right?"

"Nice 'n tight, right," Cletus agreed, but he didn't sound at all convinced.

My Grandma is always telling me I have a vivid imagination, and right then, hearing that Cletus could wind up as fish food, set my wheels into high gear. I had no problem picturing Derrick Carter—the meanest kid James had ever known—grabbing us and drowning us in that nasty mine pond. I had no trouble seeing him grinding my face into the rock floor of the mine, demanding to know what we were doing all the way up here at the Magpie Mine? All of those flashbulb pictures went off in my head and my legs suddenly got very rubbery.

James looked puzzled as I pulled out my handkerchief and tied it over my face.

"Wadda you doing?" James asked.

"In case we need to charge and bust through them, I don't want Derrick knowing who I am."

James looked at me and then yanked out his soggy bandana and put it on. We kind of resembled bandits about to rob a train. James crouched down in his football stance. It was his running back pose, waiting for the ball to be snapped. I crouched low right behind him.

* * *

It was unspoken and obvious that James should lead the charge. Not just because he was a full head and a half taller than me, but because he was the best man on the varsity football team—bigger, stronger, tougher . . . and only in the ninth grade. He can find a hole in the line when all I would see is a wad of muddy bodies with helmets. The whole team watched one time as he dragged three tacklers all the way across the goal line. But football is not a big thing for him. What we were doing right now, that's what makes James smile and get that evil look in his eye.

* * *

"If we need to blast through those guys, stay right behind me," he instructed. "Pretend we're going up the middle and straight for the end zone."

Well, I was still shaking. Trying not to breathe and be

quiet is hard when you're scared and your heart's trying to jump out of your chest. I had no idea how big Derrick was or Cletus, so I wasn't sure we'd make it if we were forced to blast through. If they were big guys, they could just grab us in the scuffle and we'd be caught. If they were our size, we might have a chance.

James answered that question when he whispered, "I can take down Derrick, but I think Cletus weighs three hundred pounds. We have surprise on our side, though, if we have to charge through."

"Three hundred pounds?" I whispered. "We're about to run into a cow!" James again had to stuff down a laugh.

Someone stopped digging again. "Think about it, Cleets. You get your share . . . if 'n you can keep yer sloppy-hinged trap shut."

The other shovel stopped working. "I do?" Cletus asked.

"You think I'd make you work for free?" Derrick said. He sounded irritated again. "Come on, Cletus, get this buried while I take a break."

A cigarette lighter clinked and then we heard the scratchy strike sound. A few seconds later cigarette smoke drifted by.

"But I'm hungry," Cletus whined. "I wanna snack."

"I told you, burgers after work," Derrick said, sounding really tired of Cletus' complaining.

It took them another ten minutes—with plenty more arguing and scuffling—until they finished up, collected their tools, and faded into the distance of the mine. I heaved a huge sigh.

We snuck out and looked at the floor of the mine. The ground was soft and sandy and their footprints were everywhere. Once in a while we heard Cletus' big laugh. It sounded miles away, so we felt safe to talk.

"They buried something, alright," James said. He knelt down and started scooping away the soft ground. For every scoop, sand and rocks fell back into the little hole he'd made.

"It's deep," I said, thinking he was going to try and dig it up with his hands.

He stopped and sat back on his heels. "Yeah . . . well, we both know the rule, right?"

I didn't answer. I knew *The Rule* . . . it would be a late night.

Chapter 3

THE RULE

I guess I should explain *The Rule*.

It started last summer when we'd been exploring an old gold processing mill. Mills are generally built on the side of a mountain with the mine shafts at the top. They use gravity to work the ore down through all the strange machines that get the gold out of the rock. They're a spider web of giant beams and posts, with all kinds of strange gizmos and things. There's lots of hidden places and little rooms too, so they're fun to explore.

When James had discovered a rusty iron door, he'd said, "It's obvious what we gotta do, Cal." But it was bolted with a fist-size lock. He'd jiggled it and yanked on it, trying every angle to see if it would break free. We both knew that sometimes those old ones will give way if you work at it, but this fat lock wasn't willing to budge. Remember the fork in the road I told you about? Where one side is fun and dangerous, and the other is just reading adventure magazines on the couch? Well, here we were, at a big fork in the road.

I walked over and checked the lock. I'm sometimes good at picking them, but this one looked solid, so I just let it drop and bang against the thick door.

"There might be dynamite in there," I warned.

"I know. That's why we're gonna get it open," he answered with kind of a wild-eyed grin. If I didn't know better, I'd have thought it was a state law for us to investigate every locked door that ever existed. He immediately started rooting around in the piles of junk, looking for anything to use as a lever. He came up with a thick steel rod.

"Hey look. A model T driveshaft," he declared.

"Gramps said old dynamite's unstable," I said.

This might be one of those times where one of us could get hurt . . . really hurt. And by us, I meant me.

James looked at me like I was nine. "Do you know what unstable is, Cal?"

"Sure I do, stupid. It's not stable."

"Right, and that means you just gotta be a little more careful with it," he said. "I'm careful with stuff."

My eyebrows shot up. I would never describe James as careful with stuff.

"I am," he argued. He knew what I was thinking.

"I think we should make a rule, Cal. We gotta find out what's behind a door before we decide what to do with it."

I felt my eyebrows squeeze together into a frown as he dragged the driveshaft to the door.

"Just cuz there might be something in there shouldn't make us not open the door." He was nodding yes, sure that he was right.

So, that's our rule—we explore, and then decide what to do with what we find.

"We gotta know what's behind that door," he said and wedged the shaft into the lock.

I have to tell you, there are times when I wonder if I'm not some kind of stupid robot from a dumb space movie. While I was blabbing on and on about Gramps and dynamite being dangerous, I'm also helping James pull back on the model T drive shaft. I'll admit it. I wanted to see what was behind that door as much as James. But then I would start quoting my mom and spout off all the ways someone would certainly get hurt.

That lock didn't have a fighting chance. Its old rivets squeezed through their holes and the big hunk of metal dropped to the dirt floor. And sure enough, dynamite is the reason it was locked. There was a case of old, moldy red sticks with "TNT" written on each one. And, of course, stenciled on the case was "DANGER—EXPLOSIVES."

"Look at that, Calvin Poag," James whispered, mysterious and in awe. He slowly drew a line in the dust under the words.

"Danger. Explosives," he said in a hushed voice.

"Yeah. I see it, James. I wonder why they wrote that on the box?" My question was thick with sarcasm and we laughed.

"Dang, no caps," James grouched after he rummaged around the little room.

"We'll figure out some other way to light 'em," he said.

An hour later, we learned what unstable meant when James tossed a stick down the hill.

After we got back up and dusted off, we high-tailed it outta there cuz the BOOM was still echoing through the canyons. Also, we had to shout back and forth for ten minutes because our ears were ringing.

* * *

So, there you go; that's how THE RULE got started and why we wind up poking our noses into places we probably shouldn't. And now, looking at that freshly dug and refilled hole by the Carter cousins, it fit squarely into the rules of THE RULE. Still, I just screwed up my mouth in my usual *I'm not so sure* sort of way.

"What about that Derrick? You said he was the meanest kid you've ever met."

"He is," James said. "But he's not gonna know." James stood up and waved his hand around the narrow shaft. "No one knows we're here, so how they gonna know who dug it up?" He smiled when he said this. James loved his own logic.

"They're going to know *someone* dug it up," I insisted. "And then they'll start looking around at everyone in Mud Lake."

"So? We're a couple a kids. He's not gonna think a couple a dumb kids went all the way up to the Magpie and then dug up whatever this is."

I listened and then nodded okay. He grinned and said, "Come on. We'll come back later with tools and stuff."

All the way back to Mud Lake, James never said a word about the quicksand adventure or his claustrophobia. I couldn't stop thinking about how it could have turned out and wanted to bring it up. Instead, we talked about what tools we'd need, and what time to meet, and what might be buried. James covered about every possibility because we were still kicking around ideas when we reached the valley floor and the main road. The more we talked and speculated on what was in that hole, the more James got quiet and kind of focused. I could see it was really eating at him that Derrick would drag his dumb cousin and something worth burying that far into the mountains.

"Why didn't he just hide it in town somewhere?" James wondered. "Or pry up the boards in a barn and hide it there? I would a just gone out in the woods somewhere and stashed it in a lava tube, and then hid the entrance."

Over and over, James came up with ideas for what he would have done, so I could see he figured it was something really special to go to that kind of trouble.

I didn't want to go back to the mine tonight because *Wild Kingdom* was on TV. Marlin Perkins and his sidekick, Jim Fowler, were my heroes . . . me and Gram were big fans. James didn't like *Wild Kingdom*, always saying, "we can go do that stuff ourselves; we don't have to watch other guys do it."

So, right now he was giving me a hard time about not wanting to go back tonight.

"Cal, what if they come back tomorrow? What if that was just a temporary hiding place or something? It's obviously loot from a robbery. You wanna miss out on recovering stolen loot? Maybe we'd get a reward or something. You ever think of that?" James asked all these questions in a rapid-fire way that made me wonder which I should answer first.

"Temporary? Would you go to all that trouble for an overnight hiding place?"

"Well, no," said James. "But if it's not, and we get it, then it's that much longer till he discovers it's gone. And that gives us more time to re-hide it and figure out what to do with it."

"It can wait a few days," I said, shrugging my shoulders.

"Good grief. This is a big deal, Cal . . . a *big deal!*"

"Maybe. Or maybe we'll be the first ones turned into fish food."

"I'm tellin' you, they won't find out, Calvin," James said, both impatient and angry.

"I don't know if you remember, *Ralph*, but there's no back door in that mine!"

"Well then, you stay home and watch other guys go on adventures. I'm gonna go find something interesting or even valuable."

"I just don't wanna sneak out," was my answer to that.

He thought for second and said, "Then come spend the night." James always had an angle. He could think of a better idea, alternate route, or way to slither out of a tight spot faster than anyone I'd ever known. Not that I've known that many people like James . . . actually none. Still, he was hard to pin down. He again had me cornered. "We don't have to sneak out," he added. "No one cares what I do. And now . . ."

James didn't finish his sentence. We both knew what he was about to say. I watched his face scrunch up into an expression that was both sorrowful and mad. I also suddenly felt sad, and looked at the ground.

"Okay," I said. "Call around eight and invite me over. No guarantees, though. You know Uncle Neal."

James brightened up a little. "We can work on our science project."

"What science project?" I asked.

"I dunno. We'll come up with something," he said while taking off on his bike.

I sat there on my bike for a moment watching him ride off ahead, thinking about what had happened that neither of us wanted to talk about.

* * *

About a month ago, James' stepdad had been killed in a trucking accident and now his family was in a very tight spot. Even though the two of them never got along, James was still a little bit sad . . . but mostly angry.

"We got no insurance, Cal," James shouted at me. "Vince didn't get us any!"

For a second, I thought he was going to start crying. It was about a week after the funeral, and I guess I'd been asking too many questions. Later, when he'd calmed down, he explained that the trucking company was thinking about suing them because Vince had been a little tipsy that night. Now I understood why James was so jumpy.

I said something to Gram about him being hard to get along with and she reminded me of how sad I'd been after Gramps died.

All I'd wanted to do was sit in his truck and be left alone. James had tried to cheer me up, and we went exploring a few times, but he knew I wasn't having much fun. Every stream or deep pool reminded me of fishing with Gramps. I was just sad all the time . . . for weeks.

So, when James had said, "no one cares what I do," he meant that his mom wasn't interested in much of anything and Vince wasn't around anymore to give him a hard time. I sighed and started toward home, trying to figure out an excuse about why I was late and all banged up.

Chapter 4

UNCLE NEAL KNOWS BEST

Sunday night was special at Gram's house. Sometimes she'd go to the evening prayer service at church, but most times she seemed to want to be with me. She'd pop popcorn and I'd sit on the couch next to her Lazy Boy (when I wasn't up fiddling with the rabbit ears to get a better picture) and we'd oouh and ahhhh at the animals and adventures on *Wild Kingdom*. Sometimes Uncle Neal would watch, but he thought the whole thing was fake and said so. Gram would shush him and tell him to go be grouchy somewhere else. Which was just fine with me. Having him phuph out snorts and crabby comments really made it hard to concentrate.

When I came in from the garage, I stopped in the laundry room and quickly shucked off my wet and muddy clothes and stuffed them in the washer. Luckily, I found my pajama bottoms in a pile of laundry and slipped them on. Gram was finishing up the dishes and Uncle Neal was looking at the Sunday paper want ads when I came waltzing in. I tried to walk a casual line through the living room, but got lassoed by Uncle Neal.

"Where have you been, Little Mister?" He didn't even look up from the paper.

"I . . . well . . ."

Then he looked up and then down at my PJ bottoms, then at my bloody face. I'd forgotten I'd gotten smacked on the head. Gram peeked around the corner and saw me.

"Calvin, what in the world happened to you?" she yelped and hurried over to me. Uncle Neal's head cocked to one side.

"Where's your regular pants?" he asked.

"Oh, ah, we got wet." I wished Mud Lake would get more mountain rain storms because it'd sure make it easier to explain why I was always wet and muddy.

"Wet? How wet? How'd you get wet?" Sometimes Uncle Neal could ask questions like he was firing them from a machine gun.

"Forget the wet pants, Neal," said Gram. "How'd you get cut, Calvin?" Uncle Neal got up to have a look.

"I, ah, hit my head," I said, sounding totally mystified as to how I'd lost a chunk of my scalp. Gram immediately wanted to take me to the doctor in White Salmon, but Uncle Neal "phooeyed" that idea.

"That'd cost a fortune, Millie," he said, and looked at my head again and pronounced, "He'll live." Which really meant that I had better live so he could grill me for days about what happened and where I had been.

"Whatever you hit, that's a nasty slash," Gram said.

"And you somehow have no idea how that happened?" Uncle Neal quizzed.

"Well, we were messing around in a (mumble) and I fell. And then (mumble) next thing I knew I was bleeding . . . a bit."

"A bit? Calvin, sit down and stop making up stories," Gram said. "Neal, get me a warm rag."

"Not until I get to the . . ."

"Neal, cut it out and get me a rag," Gram ordered. Uncle Neal jumped a little and went to get a rag.

"Calvin, I don't understand how you and James can get into so much mischief," she said and started looking me over. "And look at these scrapes and bruises."

"It's not a big deal, Gram," I muttered. The truth was I was hurting all over, but I didn't want her to know about it.

Uncle Neal returned with the warm rag and his little army medical box.

Oh no, I thought. Uncle Neal was not Gramps, who was

really good with a needle and thread, and picking out BB pellets and stuff.

Uncle Neal was giving me his stink-eye while he was threading a needle and getting out the alcohol. One caterpillar eyebrow was up and the other down. His mouth was gearing up too, watching for an open door to start his long list of questions about my whereabouts, injuries, and with whom I was cavorting. That was a new word he'd started using when he didn't want to say James Nelson. He knew who I cavorted with.

Gram would usually let out a snort laugh when he used that word. Then she'd say, "You are such a blow-hard, Neal. Cavorting? Good grief. Makes the boys sound like they're planning bank robberies."

Uncle Neal decided to start out low and easy with, "You missed supper, you know. There's a reason your Gram cooks food . . . so it's hot and ready."

"I know. I'm sorry," I mumbled. Gram was dabbing at my head and it was stinging. She stepped in to head off Uncle Neal's ambush. "Your Uncle Neal is also known to have a midnight cold chop or two."

"Mine generally start out hot and at the dinner table, with the rest of the family," he said, and dribbled alcohol on my head and mopped it up with a paper towel.

"YEOW," I screamed and jerked back.

"Neal, you're as rough as an old corn cob," Gram scolded.

"What? That doesn't hurt," he said, matter of fact. "But this will," he added and stabbed the needle into my scalp. I'm positive that he was enjoying making me flinch and wince.

I didn't want them thinking that getting hurt was a big deal, so it took everything I had not to scream out again. I know tears ran down my face, though.

"Oh for Pete's sake, you are something," Gram muttered, directed at Uncle Neal, and patted my hand. She quickly wiped away the streams running down my cheeks. My head was not at all numb and I could feel every needle poke and yank of the thread as my scalp lifted with each pull. The whole time he was stitching me back together, he was grilling me about how this happened.

"Calvin, yer gonna kill yourself running around with that Nelson kid," he said. "This would have cost fifty dollars if your Gram had run you to the hospital. I'm just glad I was here to save her that kind of extravagant expenditure."

He was looking down through his reading glasses. He reminded me of a grumpy badger. He smelled of aftershave and onions and cigarettes, three fragrances not intended to live together. I didn't answer and I don't think he really expected me to. So I just sat there biting down with my teeth while he stitched me back together.

* * *

Lots of times when I came home banged up or wet and muddy, Uncle Neal was convinced me and James had somehow stolen the whole town of Mud Lake and moved it down river somewhere. The thing is, he was generally right, sort of. We sure hadn't moved the town, but neither were we eating ice cream at the gas station soda fountain. I overheard him telling Gram one time that he knew my type of kid.

"I've dealt with his kind a hundred times, so believe you me, I know one when I see one."

"He's not a troublemaker, Neal," Gram said. "He wants to be an explorer when he grows up and study tree monkeys and learn about piranhas."

"Tree monkeys, my big toe," he snorted. "He and that

Nelson kid are gonna burn this whole puny town to the ground one day. You mark my words on the calendar."

He actually was jotting it on the calendar when I walked into the kitchen.

"Cal, take note there on the calendar," Gram said to me. "Your Uncle says that's the day you and James plan to burn down Mud Lake."

And then Gram burst out laughing. I looked at the date and then Uncle Neal. I had nothing to say. I knew me and James had no plans of burning down Mud Lake. Not intentionally, anyway.

Uncle Neal was my great uncle, and Gramps' brother. But they were almost complete opposites. Gramps had wrinkles from smiling all the time while Uncle Neal was a wrinkled up old prune from frowning. About a week after getting here, he cornered me and said that Gramps had been way too lenient and that "I couldn't pull the wool over his eyes." He started tapping me on the chest, which no one had ever done before . . . I hated that.

"I am not easily fooled or fooled with." Then he leaned in close to my face. His cigarette breath pushed me back a step. "Your kind were a dime a dozen when I was running Powder River Junior High. I knocked 'em all down to size and got 'em all on track."

I learned right off the bat that he was going to put me on the griddle any chance he got. He wanted me to sizzle like a sausage patty until I talked. I just had to figure out how to talk without saying too much. It's also when coming home after "cavorting" with James stopped being fun. Now, I had to bob-and-weave just to keep out of Uncle Neal's sights and clear of his long interrogations.

* * *

You might be wondering why I don't like to be called "Calvin" by James or Uncle Neal, but have no problems when Gram calls me by my birth name. That's because James does it to irritate, Uncle Neal stresses my full name during any round of punishment, but Grams says "Calvin" with a great deal of love . . . that's a big difference.

* * *

My surgery took a while and all I wanted to do was get upstairs and away from all the attention. I was also a bit lightheaded from the alcohol that Uncle Neal kept dabbing on my head.

Even though I knew *Wild Kingdom* was about to start, I decided I'd skip it this week. I knew Gram would understand, but when I reached the bottom of the stairs leading up to my room, Uncle Neal stopped me.

"You never did come out and say where you two outlaws were."

I looked back at him. He was closing up his little medical kit and glaring at me. Gram turned to him too.

I glanced at Gram and said, "Well, I'm a kid." I thought I'd just try something she'd said once when he was drilling me about coming home filthy. They both looked at me.

"Getting dirty is just part of being a kid." I added, hoping Gram caught that I used her explanation. Her eyes narrowed and she gave me a look that let me know she got it.

I also messed around with my face, trying on a few different expressions to help convince him that that's just the way it is. *Kids just get dirty*. I settled on a goofy smile

I'd worked up in the mirror a while back. I stood there, at the bottom of the stairs, looking at him looking at me.

It's kind of strange how my faces and expressions always make Uncle Neal frown.

* * *

Remember me telling you about my imagination getting me in trouble? Suddenly, right there at the foot of the stairs, my overactive mind kicked in and I pictured Uncle Neal and me in the bathroom working on our facial expressions for some big performance. I heard myself saying to him, "Okay, Uncle Neal, I'll smile and make sad eyes and you pinch your eyebrows together and make the corners of your mouth touch your shoulders."

So now, staring at him and imagining a different look, a small spurt of laughter shot out of my mouth. Then another one erupted. Oh no, I thought, out-of-control laughter. I couldn't turn off the image of me and Uncle Neal working together on our routine. A crazy movie had started inside my brain and I couldn't shut it off.

And then I pictured his eyebrows literally climbing up into his hair. That was it . . . now I really burst out laughing. I'd hit the top of the giggle roller coaster and now I was on the wild ride down.

Well, the pictures or movies are so real that sometimes I can't stand it. They scare me or make me laugh like I'm at an Abbott and Costello movie. It's what I call the "sleepover giggles" . . . when you're not supposed to be laughing, but that's why you're laughing, and you just can't stop.

Tears started running down my cheeks. The movie in my head—me and Uncle Neal making faces in the bathroom mirror—was hilarious. I looked over at him and through my watery eyes, I saw him making a face I'd never seen before. One of his eyebrows was practically touching his hairline and his mouth was all jacked over to the side and kind of smiling. I couldn't take it. I left the stairs and slumped over on the couch, crying with laughter. You'd think I'd just barfed all over the living room floor and was now rolling around in it.

Gram came over and sat next to me.

"Calvin, what is wrong with you?"

I looked up at her. She was all blurry from my tears and that was funny too. I flopped my head into her lap and just laughed and laughed. I finally got my breath and settled down, but I didn't dare look at Uncle Neal. I just looked up at Gram.

"Nothing," I managed to say.

She touched my forehead to check my temperature. It made it start all over again. My sides hurt and so did my face. I finally got up.

"I'm okay, Gram," I said while climbing the stairs. "Holy cow . . . sometimes my . . . wow . . . never mind."

As I disappeared into my room in the attic, I crashed down on my bed and tried to breathe. My face hurt from laughing and I was suddenly very tired. But I had to bury my face in my pillow because I again saw Uncle Neal and me in the bathroom mirror.

"Calvin?" Gram was peering at me from the top of the stairs. "You forgot your dinner."

She came the rest of the way and set it down on my desk. Then she sat down on the bed.

"You mind telling me what was so funny?" she asked with a smile.

"I can't, Gram. It's not a big deal, it's just the pictures in my head sometimes make me laugh."

I quickly grabbed my pillow and buried my face for a few seconds, to muffle my giggles and somehow not let those movies start again. A little snort did escape, but I got myself settled down.

"Well, they must have been doozies," she said.

I just nodded and Gram decided to let it go, for now.

* * *

A few months later, though, when we were at the grocery store, she asked me again what my uncontrollable laughing fit was about, and I told her what I'd seen in my mind. She looked at me and suddenly started laughing and couldn't stop either. We sat in the parking lot and just laughed till we couldn't breathe. She was so tickled by the story that she took me out for ice cream. Twice while she was sucking on her ice cream cone, she let out a snort-laugh and almost started again.

* * *

Gram handed me my dinner. "Here, eat something." She sucked in a breath and said, "Well, I wanted to tell you that Uncle Neal and I are going to White Salmon tomorrow. I have a doctor's appointment and so we'll be leaving before breakfast."

"What's wrong, Gram?" I was suddenly worried and sat up.

"Nothing really. It's no big deal. Anyway, you think you can get yourself up in the morning and fix your own breakfast?"

I nodded, yes. Right then the phone rang downstairs.

"Sure, Gram. I'll just have cereal."

"Calvin, telephone," Uncle Neal yelled from the living room. Gram rolled her eyes. "It's a good thing your room isn't in the barn. He'd blow out a lung."

A spurt of laughter burst from my mouth. Her eyes got real big and she held up her finger. "Put a cork in that, buster. If I'm not in on the joke, I won't tolerate solo giggle-fests, you hear?" She smiled.

* * *

It was James on the phone.

"Tonight? Sure, I'll ask . . ."

I took a deep breath.

"Gram, can I spend the night at James'? We're doing a science project and we wanna work on it."

"It's Sunday night, Calvin," Uncle Neal barked out. "And you're injured."

Gram reached the bottom of the stairs. "A science project for school? I don't see why not."

"It's a school night, Millie," Uncle Neal interrupted.

I stood there for five minutes while they duked it out about me spending the night. But the fact that they were going to White Salmon in the morning kind of clinched it.

"Finish your dinner before you leave," Gram said as I hurried up the stairs.

Chapter 5

AN OVERNIGHTER TO REMEMBER

The Nelson kids had a reputation for being wild and unsupervised. Which is basically true; how wild depending on their age. The baby was missing one morning and they found her crawling across the road with their sheepdog. And there was the time Beth, who's around three, pretended she was driving Mrs. Nelson's Chevy, but somehow got it out of gear and it rolled into the corner of the house.

Since Mud Lake and the surrounding area has a pretty small population, there's only one school . . . and the Nelson kids definitely have a reputation.

The twins, Noodle and Rusty, who just turned five, brought some of James' firecrackers to kindergarten and were showing everyone at lunch how to light and throw them before they exploded. Two kids ended up in the nurse's office.

And then there's twelve-year-old Pepper, who often makes me nervous and gets in fights . . . usually standing up for the little kids. Uncle Neal claims that Pepper has her very own chair in the principal's office because she's there so much.

James, of course, is my age—fourteen—and I guess it could be argued that he's the wildest Nelson of all. Naturally, Uncle Neal doesn't care much for my friendship with James and tells me whenever he can. Gram, though, does care for James and she trusts me. Even so, it's a constant point of discussion around the house.

* * *

As it turned out, I got to watch *Wild Kingdom* after all. At least some of it. The Nelsons lived outside town and their TV reception was even worse than ours. I took a stab at some of the techniques that I used on our TV and everyone was glad that I was getting rid of the snow on the screen. Me and James pretended to go to bed around ten, but laid around waiting. I suddenly noticed something slip under the door.

"What's that?" I said and got up to get it. It was a note written in pencil. I read out loud, "I know you guys are doing something tonight. I want to come too."

"Pepper," James grumbled. He got up and jerked open his door. Pepper stood there, with her mouth tight and her eyes narrowed down to slits.

"Come in here," he whispered to her. "Wadda you doin'?"

"I wanna come with you guys," she whispered back.

"We're not doin' nothin'," James lied.

"You are too. How come you're sleeping over on a Sunday night?" she asked, directed more at me.

Before I could come up with something, James said, "We're working on our school project."

Pepper glanced around his room. "What project? I know you're doing something and I wanna come with . . ."

* * *

Right after Pepper got her big-girl bike, a pink Schwinn

Spitfire, things changed for me and James. Before the Spitfire, she was just one of his little sisters and we could get away from her if we needed to. Which was fine with me because too often I caught her ogling me. James thought that was hilarious and teased me about it.

"What if you married Pepper?" he popped off one time. "You'd be my brother-in-law." He fell over with laughter at that idea. I just stood and looked at him on the ground. I felt a little bit of barf attempting to come up my throat and, after that, started trying to avoid even being in the same room with Pepper. Then she started trying to get the other girls at school to chase me, so she could then be part of the herd and chase me too. I had to come up with new lunch plans to keep from feeling like an African deer being run down by lions.

So, with her new bike, Pepper started showing up when me and James were planning a trip. She'd have her Nancy Drew sleeping bag tied to the handle bars with twine and her crummy little knapsack full of who knows what. James would tell her she wasn't coming and she'd get pouty or threaten to tell their mom that he was being mean. And, it seemed like she was always watching me. I think she was hoping I'd say, "Sure, come along. Maybe you can chase me on your little girly bike."

We decided to let her tag along a few times, but we just rode around the valley or sat on the rim and stared into the Salmon River. She got bored and figured out we were just teasing her. For a little seventh grader, she started reading the signs when we were really brewing up an adventure and it got harder and harder for us to get away by ourselves.

* * *

Pepper leaned against the door and glared at us. "I'm going with you," she whined. I noticed she wasn't in her usual peddle pusher pants and tee shirt. She was dressed for cold travel. Long pants and a sweatshirt.

"No, you're not, Pepper, because we're not doing anything," James said for the umpteenth time. "You need ta mind yer own beeswax."

"Well, what are you doing, then?" she asked. I heard it in her voice. She was going to start pouting. I suddenly spied James' army pack on the floor. If she sees it, she'll know we're up to something, I thought.

"I told you, we're working on a science project for school," James added and grabbed his science book. She looked back at him and I casually inched the pack under the bed. James flipped open the book and stabbed his finger at some random page. "Frog hearts. We're dissecting frogs and me and Cal have done that before, so the teacher asked us to talk about it. Right Cal?"

I nodded, and glanced at the book. It was open to the moon's orbit around the earth. I took the book and held it so Pepper couldn't see it.

"Yup, frog hearts are not easy to dissect," I said. "Very small and delicate. One wrong move and your frogger is a goner."

James looked at me and burst out laughing. Pepper's eyes turned to thin slits again and her mouth jerked over to one side. I knew that face. It was her *your lyin' to me* face. Uncle Neal gives me his version of it all the time. Her hands suddenly shot up and parked on her hips.

"Eh, the frog's already dead, Calvin," Pepper sneered. "You two are makin' fun of me." She stomped her foot.

"Ah, come off it, Pepper," James said. She just stared at him, and he stared back. "Ah, okay," he said in a very low voice. He looked at me and screwed up his mouth. "We're gonna catch some catfish tonight up at the pond."

As James waved his hand in the general direction of the old mill, Pepper slumped to one side.

"On a school night?"

"No one'll be up there," James said. "We're not dump-heads, you know."

"Well, I still wanna come."

"Will you cut it out, Pepps," James said, trying to be quiet.

"You're whispering," she said in a loud whisper. "I know you're doing something because yer whispering, and I'm coming with you."

"If me and Cal wanna do something, it's because we got somethin' we gotta do. Got it? But we don't. And when we do got somethin' to do, we're sure not gonna tell you. Now go to bed and quit bugging us."

As James waved his hand in a *go-away* gesture, Pepper looked at me and I thought maybe she might start crying. Instead, she turned and left his room, slamming the door. James blew out some air and flopped back on his bed.

"Girls," he muttered.

* * *

We decided to turn out the light and fake sleeping until Mrs. Nelson went to bed. An hour later, we were on the bumpy dirt road to the Magpie mine. And three hours later we were hiding in the trees making sure no one was around.

"I think the coast's clear," James whispered. We stepped out and started toward the mine's black mouth. I was checking the ground for any more tracks.

"I only see the one set of tire tracks," I said. They were still fresh in the soft dirt. We stuffed our bikes into some bushes and walked into the black hole. Even with our army surplus flashlights, the blackness seemed to swallow us. All we'd brought were two folding army shovels and our rope. I was bugged we'd not brought enough tools. I'd said that from the start. The trouble was we'd needed to leave James' house in a hurry, before Pepper or someone heard us. James wouldn't let me go out into their barn and see if there was something else that might be handy.

"What if we need to break into whatever it is we're digging up?" I asked.

James held up his shovel. "We'll bash it open," he said. "We can handle it, Cal."

"I hope so. It's a long ride back if we need something," I muttered.

At the spot where Derrick and Cletus had buried whatever it was, everything looked the same as when we'd left. We started digging, but it didn't take long for James to get annoyed with me for signaling to stop and listen. I couldn't help it; our shovel sounds were just as loud as when Derrick and Cletus had been digging.

CLUNK. SWISH. CLUNK. SWISH . . . we dug until we heard a distinct THUD. We'd hit something.

"Bingo!"

We got down on our knees and tried to pull the sand out with our hands. The trouble was the soft sand and rocks kept falling back into the hole. It took a while longer to finally see something.

"There's a handle," I said and grabbed a metal handle that was bolted to the side. "It's some kind of chest or strong box."

"Yeah," he agreed, pulling on the sand to clear the box. "There's the other handle."

We started tugging, but the box was really heavy and down in the hole. We caved in a side and both of us pulled it up and out. We sat back and looked at the wooden box.

"You're right, it's a strong box," James said.

It was made of thick wood and held together with iron straps and rivets. Each corner was steel too. James grabbed the lock and shook it, then let it drop.

"That'll be hard to bust open," he grumbled and then hit it with his shovel. The loud BANG echoed back up the mine shaft and came back. That instantly made me nervous and I looked back up the tunnel. I didn't hear anything, so I looked at the lock. It was very old. I dug my Swiss knife out of my pocket, opened the pick, and pulled out the tweezers.

"That won't work," James said. "It's too old for that kind of picking. Let's just drag it outta here and hide it. We can come back with a crowbar."

I grabbed an end and lifted.

"That'll take us hours," I grunted. I bent down and started working the pick and tweezers into the lock. "I'll just . . ."

CLICK . . . the lock popped open.

"You did it," James said, all smiles.

We flipped back the lid. My eyes flew open and James' jaw dropped.

"Whoa," he whispered.

The light from our flashlights reflected back in our faces from hundreds of coins. I leaned in and looked, then picked up a gold coin. James scooped up a handful and let them fall through his fingers. He laughed and did it again. The coins made a thick clinking sound as they fell back down into the chest to rejoin the hundreds of other coins.

"We're pirates," he said and then growled "arrrrr."

I scooped up a double handful and let them fall through my fingers too. We scooped and scooped and then sat back and just stared at the little chest of treasure. I again grabbed a handle and gave the chest a little tug.

"What are we gonna do with this? We can't carry it on our bikes," I said.

He stared at it. "Let's bury it at the bottom of Shaft #3

and we'll come back with sacks. We'll keep making trips till we get it all." Well, that was one idea, I thought. I'll bet you can guess my next thought.

"Who do ya think this really belongs to?"

"How should I know," James snapped as he tested the chest's weight. "Heavy, but we can do it," he added and motioned for me to grab the other end.

"It's probably stolen, is what I'm getting at," I said. I got up and just stood there.

"Probably," he agreed. "That's why we need to hide it, cuz maybe we can be heroes."

I let that idea roll around in my head for a second. Any time there was a chance for James to be a hero, it always got his attention. It'd happened a few times in the past for us, and we even got in the papers. I didn't really care for that part, having people I didn't know coming up and wanting me to tell what happened and all. Saving the day and riding in a police car, though, had been cool. If this chest was stolen—and I figured it was, after listening to Derrick talk about the whole thing being his "special project"—I decided hiding it from him was our best option.

I grabbed my end and lifted. James was right . . . it was heavy. "Okay, maybe we can be heroes again," I said. He laughed and we started lugging it up the shaft.

We hadn't gone very far when I stopped. I set my end down and he had to stop too.

"What?" James asked.

"Smell that?" I whispered. James sniffed.

"Cigarettes," he whispered. "I don't believe it. It can't be them."

"You wanna hang around and see?" I asked. "I don't think we can make it to Shaft #3."

"We need to go down," he said, tilting his head back toward the nasty pond. My mouth screwed up. I hated that idea, but that was about all we had at the moment.

"You wanna stand here and think about it some more?"

he asked. I didn't and grabbed my end.

Running with a sixty-pound chest of coins is not easy. And when we stopped at the hole to grab our shovels and packs, it got even harder.

As we were hustling along, following our crazy, bouncing flashlight beams through the gloom, James said, "This solves our problem."

"What problem?"

"Our money problems. Wait'll my mom sees all this. She'll cry."

"Stop for a second," I said, puffing and gasping for air. "I need to get the blood back into my hand."

"Okay, but not long."

Quietly as possible, we put down the chest and both took some deep breaths.

"James . . ."

"Cal," he interrupted. "Finders keepers."

"I was just going to say . . ."

"I know what you were going to say. Now, come on."

James picked up his end of the treasure chest . . . and I followed his lead.

Chapter 6

NEVER TRUST A THIEF

I decided to let my ideas alone for a while. At the moment, we needed to escape Derrick and Cletus. Besides, I had to figure out exactly what James was thinking and if I wanted to be a part of it.

We rounded the corner and there it was, the pond, blocking our way from escape.

"Well, here we are," I said. "We're sure not swimming anywhere with this lug."

"Nope, that's for sure," James muttered. He aimed his light into the water. We could see rocks and mud and where our feet had already made shoe size dimples in the bottom.

"But we can sink it," he said and nodded.

"And never see it again," I said. "Remember . . ."

I decided not to bring up him getting stuck in quicksand, but could tell by the way his mouth tightened that he also was thinking about the treasure sinking forever into the muck.

"Or, we could tie it off so it doesn't sink into the mud or quicksand or whatever it was," I added. I could tell instantly that he loved my plan because he slugged me in the shoulder, which meant "great idea."

While I wrapped and twisted the rope around a handle, I thought out loud, "Wadda we do after we sink it?"

"We swim, dummy. When Derrick and Cletus see their chest is gone, it's gonna be a rodeo, for sure."

I looked at him, then out over the water. Everything in me froze. Even my breathing seemed to stop.

"It's swim, Cal, or try to explain to Derrick and his monkey cousin why we're up here in the middle of the night and there's a big hole where their chest was."

I rolled my eyes away from the water and up to look at him. The options were bad and worse.

In Sunday school class, I'd heard that Jesus had walked on water one time during a storm. I sure wished I knew how to do that, because right now it'd sure come in handy.

James was lifting his end of the chest. "Come on." He started to move toward the water.

"Wait, we need to . . ." I didn't finish because my mind was back picturing the chest four feet in the muck. "We still need to find something to tie it off," I said and looked around the narrow mine shaft. "Look at that pipe running across the water." An old steam pipe was bolted to the stone wall and ran off into the blackness and around the corner in the shaft.

"They might not notice a rope tied to that," I said.

"I dunno, Cal," James said as he gripped the end of the rope and started out into the water. He didn't go very far because there were some bolts and clamps in the wall that he was able to grab. He got out over the deeper part of the water and threaded the rope over the pipe. It took everything we had to lift that chest out into the water, and the pipe was bending a little from the weight. Also, the rope was cutting into our hands. The chest finally hit bottom and we tied it off to a bolt and stepped back.

"Looks okay," James said as he left the water. "It's such a mess everywhere that I don't think anyone will even notice."

"HEY," a voice yelled from way back in the mine. "I know's yer here!"

Whoever it was had just discovered our theft. He went quiet for a few seconds, probably trying to decide what to do. Then he shouted, "You better hold up!"

"I think it's Cletus," I whispered.

"Where's Derrick?" James asked. He didn't wait around to discuss it further, he just waded right back in and started swimming, trying to hold his flashlight from getting wet. I froze at the water's edge. He glanced back and stopped to tread water. "Come on, there's nothing down there to get ya," James whispered.

Again, he knew what I was thinking. There'd been plenty of times where he'd just dive in and swim across a stream or pond or dive underwater to explore this or that, while I'd take fifteen minutes looking for another way across.

"I ain't gettin' cornered down here by Derrick Carter," James said with emphasis.

I punched the air and shoved myself into the black water. The shivers that suddenly hit me weren't just from the icy cold water. It was also from those pictures and articles in my *National Geographics* I told you about, the ones about the giant crocodiles.

I heard Cletus getting closer. You could tell he was not used to running. "You think you can . . ." he shouted and huffed. It's just him, I thought.

"Keep swimming, Cal!"

James had slowed down, so we were side by side.

A light suddenly appeared on the walls and we clicked off ours and swam faster. The light jigged and jagged because the person was running. Then he raced around the corner and almost ran into the water.

"OOOOFF," he grunted as he fell, then scrambled to his feet. He swung his light around, trying to find us, but we'd both ducked underwater. I could hold my breath longer than James. When I came up for air, he was facing away from the light, and went back under. I gulped a breath and did the same. The next time I came up for air, James was up and looking back. The person was gone and we were in complete darkness. It took everything in me not to panic. I heard James stuttering and then his groping hands found me and started hauling me forward. He banged into the jagged wall and started using it as our guide. I could hear my teeth chattering from the icy water . . . and fear.

Finally, our feet hit bottom. I didn't dare trust it though. I didn't want to sink into some sandy goo, so I kind of slithered up the bank till it was dry.

"Made it," James whispered.

"Yeah. Made it where?"

I heard him messing with his light. "I need to dry out the inside," he was saying.

I could hardly move my fingers, but I got my handkerchief out of my pocket and wrung it out.

"Here, it's not dry, but it'll help."

His hand finally found mine and grabbed it. I heard clicking and rubbing and blowing, and then his light came on. He quickly tucked it under his shirt. He looked at me and grinned.

"Look at us," he laughed as quietly as he could.

We were both all red. "Minerals in the water," I said. I rubbed my arm and it didn't really rub off. I grabbed the handkerchief back and rubbed my face and mouth.

"Get it off your mouth, James," I ordered. He did.

"Wow," he whispered. "We did it. Now, we gotta . . ." He looked around down the mine. "Maybe there's another spur." He shot his light down the tunnel in front of us, but the blackness ate it up.

"Hey, the cigarette smoke was coming down the mine," I said. "So that means it was following a small breeze."

I held up my wet hand. "It's colder on this side," I said and pointed back up the mine.

"Yeah, okay, let's go."

We headed off at a light-footed trot and almost missed a little side shaft. We skidded to a stop.

"Wait," I said and moved ten feet past the spur. Then back. "Feel that? This little shaft's where the air's going."

I never really knew if James appreciated my scientific way of looking at things. But I always figured that was my side of the team. He always charged ahead and I tried to head-off us getting killed. I know I'm sometimes a slow poke or a scaredy cat, but it was me just trying to think things out. James would just take it or leave it and keep going. Like right now. He smacked my shoulder and said, "Let's go!" and we took off in our new direction.

The little vent tube we found was steep and only big enough for us to go single file. It took about fifteen minutes for us to find that it ended around the side of the mountain. It didn't have much of an opening either; we had to shinny through. When we popped out into the open air, we both started to shake from the cold and being wet.

"Why was Cletus here by himself?" James asked. We were hurrying to get back to the mine's front entrance and running helped warm us up.

"To steal the loot they'd just buried, I bet," I said.

"If he is, there's gonna be some fireworks when Derrick finds out," James said.

When we got close to the mine entrance, we hid in the underbrush. Everything was quiet and no one seemed to be around. But parked near the entrance was a run-down, late fifties Plymouth with huge tail fins and strips of chrome. In the dark, someone who didn't know cars might think a spaceship had landed and skidded to a stop in the woods.

"Fifty-eight Belvedere," I said.

"Wadda ya think?" James asked.

"I think we should make a break for it and get outta here before Cletus, or whoever that is, comes out."

James didn't say anything. I could tell he wasn't onboard with my suggestion.

"What if he comes out with the chest?" James finally asked.

"Well, I guess he gets it and we go home?" I was about done with this late-night adventure. I was freezing and Cletus now knew someone had got to that chest before him. No telling what he might do.

"If he finds it, he finds it, James. What are we gonna do about it?"

James suddenly hunkered down further into the scrub maples. I could almost see the wheels in his head grinding away.

"Look," he said, "just inside the entrance. There. See him?"

Sure enough, someone was lurking in the shadows. He didn't come right out, but we saw his movements. He was slowly walking from one side to the other, trying to stay hidden.

Finally, he just stepped out and looked around. I hadn't actually seen Cletus up till then. He was big! His thick shoulders were bent and he moved with a strange shuffle.

"He walks like a bear," I whispered.

"Yeah, don't wanna get a hug from him," James added.

Cletus stopped and sucked on his cigarette. The tip made a bright orange dot in the night, and we could see him blow out big puffs of smoke in the moonlight. He was looking for us, but not willing to wander far from the Plymouth. "Who's out there?" he grumbled at the forest. Of course we didn't answer.

"We should hoot or howl, or something. Just to scare him," James whispered.

"I think we should just wait till he leaves," I murmured.

Cletus paced around a little more and then climbed into the Plymouth. As he was backing up, the car's lights passed our bikes and he stopped. We hadn't really hidden them as good as we should.

Cletus jumped out and walked into the light and jerked my bike from the bushes.

"Kids," he yelled. The word echoed through the trees and died away. He yelled out, "You get on out here!"

"Should we go?" James asked. I looked at him and he snickered.

"What?" I asked.

"He said for us to get on out. I'm just wonderin' if we should," James repeated.

I snickered too and gave him a little slug in the shoulder and he had to stifle a laugh in his shirt. We suddenly stopped, though, when Cletus held my bike up over his head and threw it to the ground. I started to jump up, but James grabbed my arm and held me down. The Schwinn was a present from my dad, right after he'd moved me up to Mud Lake.

I knew he'd felt bad about the way things were going in Portland and that my mom and him were fighting like cats in a sack. So I think the bike was his way of trying to say he was sorry, and that I had to leave my school and friends for a while. It didn't matter why he'd given it to me; I thought it was the greatest thing since spinning lures. It was a Schwinn Corvette three speed, and no one around Mud Lake had one.

So when Cletus started stomping on the spokes and wheels and picked it up and threw it down again, I almost started to cry. Luckily, James had me tight by the arm because he knew how much that bike meant to me. We watched as Cletus gave James' bike the same treatment.

The whole time he was destroying our bikes, he was growling and shouting out things we couldn't understand. A few times he stopped to catch his breath and looked around the hills and forest.

"Wow," James whispered. "He's crazy, for sure. My mom's always said Carmelita Carter's crazy. Says she's 'certifiable,' but I don't know what that means."

"It means she should be locked up in a padded cell," I muttered. "Cletus should be locked up too."

Knowing what "certifiable" meant made me instantly sad. My dad had my mom taken to Dammasch, the state's mental hospital, just before he moved me up to live with Gram and Gramps. He came home from work one day and she was throwing rocks at the neighbor's house and screaming that "they were trying to get her babies." The neighbor lady had tackled her and they were wrestling around on the front lawn while me and my little sister watched and cried. So I knew what certifiable meant. And to me, Cletus was a candidate.

He yanked out his cigarette pack and lit up another one. He blew out a big cloud of smoke and gave our bikes a couple more stomps and then stuffed himself into the Plymouth and left. I jumped up to run down there, but James grabbed my shirt.

"Hold up," James said. "Let's wait to see if he's a trickster."

I slumped back down to wait. I doubted if Cletus knew how to trick anybody. Still, I waited. It didn't matter, though. I knew our bikes were ruined. They were. I grabbed mine and tried rolling it, but the wheels were so bent they just jammed in forks. I threw it back down and started walking. I was so mad I couldn't say anything.

I'd wanted to hide them down the road a ways when we first got to the mine, but James, as usual, wouldn't listen to me. He just kept pushing forward, and I followed along. And now, here we were, walking home, wet and cold.

"That was smart of Cletus, smashin' up our bikes like that," James said when he caught up with me. James couldn't resist a good plan, even if it was by someone else and now meant we had to walk fifteen or twenty miles.

"Brilliant," I agreed. I sure didn't mean it, though.

James seemed unfazed by having his bike smashed. He was already trying to figure out when we should come back and finish the job of getting that chest of coins.

"Hey, we can go back in there right now, get the chest, and hide it better." He was looking at me, gauging my interest in that concept.

"Forget it. What if that's the trap? What if he smashed our bikes and is waiting somewhere close to see if that's what we'll do."

I wasn't going back in the mine. Not tonight anyway. I kept walking.

"Nah," James said. "If that was his plan, he'd a showed up by now. He's halfway back to the Carter's house."

"If Cletus is pulling a fast one on Derrick," I said with a bite in my voice, "why would he be going back there?"

"Maybe he plays dumb and says it's stolen," James said.

"That won't be hard," I grumbled. "It is stolen. Besides, he's only running on half his spark plugs." James snort-laughed.

"Derrick's gonna figure it out," he said, "and Cletus is going to be cooked."

I was done talking about Cletus. I was freezing.

James knew I was mad and decided to let it drop . . . for now anyway. He let me walk ahead of him and be by myself.

All I could think about right then was Uncle Neal and the list of questions he'd be asking about my bike and why's it all smashed up? He'd keep me busy for a week with all his questions.

"HEY," James suddenly shouted.

I didn't stop or turn around.

"Cal! Stop! Look!"

I looked back to see James pulling a girl's Schwinn out of the bushes and into the moonlight. "It's Pepper's bike," he said.

I hustled back to him. Its spokes were also smashed and the front wheel bent. A shiver ran up my spine. "She followed us," I whispered and looked around the woods.

"Then, where is she?" James asked. He also looked off into the woods and then shouted, "PEPPER!"

I about jumped out of my skin. Shouting was a terrible idea.

"Cletus," I muttered, "He somehow found her and nabbed her."

"That's what he did, Cal. Cletus saw her and . . . PEPPER," he yelled again. There was no answer. Just "PEPPER" echoing through the trees, which gave me the willies.

"Come on." He limped her wounded bike into the forest and hid it in some brush. "We need to hit the gas," he said and started off at a trot.

We'd jogged down the road about a quarter mile when suddenly headlights turned on and blinded us. We both dashed off into the woods and hunkered down.

"You fellers ain't gettin' away with it," Cletus shouted. "I got yer little girl here in this here car trunk. She's comin' home with me, if 'n you don't get straight with ME!" He sounded mad. He slapped the trunk with his fist and we heard a muffled YELP from inside.

"Now what?" I whispered.

"Let's rush 'im," James suggested.

"Are you kidding? You were right, he is three hundred pounds. He'd just maul us and then stick us in the trunk with Pepper."

"Where's my things?" Cletus screamed in near panic. "I can't mess around wid you two!"

Cletus walked closer to the edge of the trees. "She might run outta air in there," he yelled out.

James looked at me. "You get around the other side of the car and see if you can distract him."

"With what?"

"I dunno, figure something out," he snapped.

"Well, I got a great idea. Let's give him that chest of coins and then everybody's happy."

James didn't answer for a few seconds. He just stared out at Cletus. "I guess that's what we gotta do," he mumbled. "We might never see anything like that ever again, ya know."

I looked at him.

"Pepper's in his trunk, James. We might not see her ever again," I said emphatically.

He scrunched up his mouth. "Get ready to run for it," he whispered. Then he shouted out to Cletus, "Don't matter! Don't know who that is you got in your trunk!"

Cletus took three big steps back to the car and smashed his fist down on the trunk again. Pepper screamed "help" this time. She started kicking the lid and Cletus yelled at her. "You cut it out!"

"Let's tell him we'll make the trade. That'll get him back to the mine and maybe we can figure something out," I said. James thought about that idea, then shouted, "Not gonna help you 'less you let that little girl out!"

"Gotta get my stuff first," Cletus shouted back.

"You go back to the mine," James shouted. "We'll be there!"

Cletus paced and smoked and thought. Then he climbed back in the Plymouth and started up the road.

"Did he buy it?" I asked. The road was narrow and he'd need to find a place to turn around, so we didn't know if he was going to the mine or searching out a wide spot.

"Dunno," James said. "Let's go see."

We started running up the road behind him, going slow and checking that he wasn't hiding around the next curve. James was obviously thinking of angles.

"Maybe we can work a split," he said excitedly. "We get some and he gets some. He might not even really know what's in that chest. Maybe it's been locked and he's never seen inside. We could open it and dump out some coins and relock it."

I just shook my head. This was getting out of control.

We snuck up on the mine and there was Cletus, pacing around the beat-up Plymouth. He looked on edge.

"If you can create a distraction, I can slip in the mine," James whispered.

"Again with the distraction. It's not gonna work, James. You can't lift that box by yourself . . . I don't think."

"I think I can," James said. "I have to. I can drag it. What else we gonna do? Lead him down there and then he drowns us to keep us quiet?"

That sounded a real possibility.

"I need to get the chest and then we can bargain for Pepper," he said. I just nodded and we split up. I went back the way we'd come a little ways to give James time to get close to the entrance.

"What am I going to do?" I whispered to myself. "I could charge the car and wrestle him down, and then get away. Right, knock over a giant . . ."

I talked and argued with myself until I figured James was inside the mine. I found a good hiding place where I could still get to the road if I needed.

"You ready to start talkin'?" I shouted in my low, gruff voice.

"Yeah," Cletus snarled back. "Are you?"

"Here's the plan," I shouted. "You're gonna let that little girl out and walk her over to those rocks." I was watching him from my hiding place. He looked around. There were rocks everywhere.

"No," I yelled, trying to sound mad. "The other rocks; over to the right." He looked off to his right. "My right, your left," I instructed.

I wanted to sound annoyed and I wanted to confuse him. It worked so well that I almost laughed. Cletus was looking all around the area trying to decide which way I was meaning.

"Oh, for the love of Mike! Just get 'er outta that trunk and over away from the car," I yelled, trying to sound very angry. The truth was I was very scared.

He stalled.

"I needs ta see my chest. You fellers said you had my chest up here. You want this little girl, I needs ta see my chest." I could tell he was getting very frustrated, so I decided to just shut up for a little while and let him worry about what was next. My suddenly going quiet made him fidgety. He opened the trunk and grabbed Pepper and held her up. She wiggled and fought like a sixty-pound salmon I'd once caught. She went kind of crazy and started wiggling and squirming and kicking. But she was no match for Cletus.

"I's gots her, you twerps! I can do what I want with her."

Pepper bit him and he yelped, so he shoved her back in the trunk and slammed the lid.

"I'm gonna make you a deal," I hollered. "Fair trade for her and half what's in the chest." Seeing Pepper scared and jammed into an old car trunk made me want to speed up her rescue.

"No deal, Bub! It's mine! I buried it!"

"Well, you don't got it now."

He didn't know what to say to that and paced around a bit. Then he lit another cigarette and blew out great puffs of smoke into the cold air. They reminded me of how cold I was. I was shaking and my teeth were chattering.

"Sometimes you gotta make a deal when you want something real bad," I yelled out to him.

"It's mine and I want it back!" Cletus actually stomped his foot on the ground.

"No, you and Derrick buried it, Cletus. I seen ya."

Cletus suddenly froze and cocked his head. I could tell by how he stiffened up that the wheels were turning in his head . . . no matter how rusty those wheels might be.

"How you know my name?"

"I know you're up here double crossin' Derrick. That's what I know."

Cletus froze with his cigarette half way to his mouth. Then he started rubbing his chin and quickly mussed up his hair, as if messy hair might help him think better.

"So, how 'bout we work a deal here and Derrick won't ever need to know?" I tried to sound cheerful at what a great idea this was. "Keeps you outta hot water."

His body posture changed again and he hunkered down. I wondered why he was trying to make himself small. For a second I wondered if he was going to charge the forest and find me. He started to back up and slowly he opened the driver's door.

"Where ya goin'?" I yelled, but he didn't answer. He suddenly jumped in and started the Plymouth and tore out of the clearing and off down the road, throwing dust and gravel in a ten-foot arch.

Oh no, I thought. I rushed out from my hiding spot in time to see his tail lights disappear around a corner. I ran to the mine and yelled as loud as I could down the tunnel.

"James," I yelled. No answer. My voice was swallowed up by the bends and sand and jagged walls. I yelled his name again, only louder. Again, no answer. I started to pace the clearing trying to think of a plan. I didn't have a flashlight, so I couldn't go down the mine. I didn't have any matches, so no fire. Then I spied it. A tiny dot of light in the dirt. Cletus had tossed down his half smoked cigarette when he escaped. I grabbed it and looked around for anything flammable.

"Pine needles," I almost shouted, and made a big pile of them five feet inside the mine's entrance. I gently puffed the cigarette into life. Having my lips on Cletus' cigarette about made me gag, but I had to make some fire and smoke. I held a handful of needles and stuck the glowing dot in the middle and pulled on the cigarette. Its glow quickly ignited the needles and I set them with the others. I softly blew on them and they burst into flame.

I don't care how brave you are, flames in a dark place always make people feel better. And that's how I instantly felt. I ran around and gathered up more needles and chunks of dry wood. It only took a minute for me to have a little fire going. I needed smoke though, so I pulled a few sticks out and let them sputter. I hoped the smoke would travel down the mine and get James' attention. I was sure the smell of a camp fire would make him wonder what was going on and hurry back to see. I was right. Twenty minutes later his flashlight appeared out of the gloom.

"What's going on?" He was all out of breath and looked

confused.

"Cletus tore off."

"Why? What happened?"

"Not sure, but I think I scared him off. I told him we knew that he'd been up here with Derrick, but that we could split the chest and he wouldn't get in any trouble. No one had to know. Then, he just jumped in the car and tore off."

James dropped down and sat on a rock.

"And he took Pepper," he said, his mind obviously at full throttle. "He's gonna tell the Carters that two kids took Derrick's chest, and he caught this little girl running around up there, and captured her as a hostage."

"I don't think he's going to say that, James. How's he going to explain the treasure chest part of this? And why he was up here?"

James could see that I had a good point.

"Dunno, he's in a serious pickle jar, for sure."

"I don't think he'll say anything about the chest, James. I bet he just dumps Pepper off somewhere and hopes it all goes away."

"Dumps Pepper off somewhere?" James asked. "Alive?"

My eyebrows arched up. Alive? That hadn't even crossed my mind when I said "dump Pepper off somewhere." I meant open the trunk and toss her out, and Cletus telling her to keep her mouth shut. So, now, my mouth fumbled around for something to say.

"Well, ah, yeah, sure . . . . alive." The thought of big, dumb, frightened Cletus trying to solve this very simple problem, and Pepper now a part of that problem, had me worried.

James stood up and started pacing the clearing. "He thinks he's been caught getting into Derrick's loot. We gotta get going," he shouted and took off running down the road.

When I caught up with him, I asked, "Did you get the chest lifted up?"

He shook his head. "Just barely got started when I smelled the smoke."

Even though we ran a lot of the way, we didn't get close to town until around noon. We were both dog tired and hid out for a while to rest and figure out what to do next. It barely crossed my mind that we were missing school, but what could we do?

James wanted to charge on up to the Carters, thinking that's where Cletus would have gone. I was still thinking that Cletus might just dump Pepper somewhere, so I wanted to go to James' house first to see if she was there. If she was safe at home, we could relax a little. For once James agreed that seeing if Pepper was home was a quick and easy step for us.

So, we slunk around the backroads and snuck across the fields. His mom's car was gone and we stole in the back door. The house was empty. The pit of my stomach crashed with that sickening empty feeling. I knew James felt the same. Why couldn't she just be here . . . safe?

"I think he took her to the Carter's house," James said. "We gotta get up there." He paced around the kitchen, stuffing a slice of bread into his mouth and handing me one too.

"How?" I asked, my mouth full of bread.

"I dunno yet."

"I gotta be home when Gram and Uncle Neal get there, or I'll get skinned."

James just looked at me. "My sister's been kidnapped by Cletus the man-bear, and yer not gonna help?"

Yes, I nodded.

"Tonight. We'll go look tonight," I offered. "Let's rest a little first, and figure out how we're going to get up there."

"Well, I can't stick around here," he said. "If Mom doesn't see me, she'll just figure Pepper's with me. Let me come sleep in your barn."

James sleeping in our barn was how our next plan

developed, and how we found ourselves deeper in a pot of steaming hot Carter stew.

Chapter 7

LEO THE BLUE HEALER

When we got to Grams, James hid in the barn and I went in the house. The car wasn't in the garage and Uncle Neal had left a list of instructions about this and that.

Leo, our bouncy Blue Healer, had met us at the barn and now sat staring at me. He wanted his dinner, but I just wanted to rest. I sat at the table and stared out the window at Mount Adams. It always reminded me of a huge pyramid. The mountain was so close that it filled a lot of the window frame. We hadn't gotten a good snow yet, so it was half rocks and half last year's ice. Somewhere, dug in along its base was the Magpie mine, with a little chest of coins sunk in a nasty pond, the start of all this trouble.

"Where in the world was Pepper?" I said to myself. Leo answered with his thumping tail. I looked at him. "Wherever she is, she's probably scared out of her socks," I said to him. I wanted to get going to find her just as much as James did, but I was so tired and hungry and needed to rest. I quickly made a couple PBJs and ate one. I decided I'd give James the other one when we started out. However are we were going to do that? We had no bikes, no car, no nothing . . . and we needed to get way out of town. The problem made me even more tired and I flopped down on the couch. My watch said three. I figured Gram and Uncle Neal would be home soon.

"I'll just close my eyes for a few minutes," I muttered to Leo, "and then get your dinner."

Instantly, I conked out . . .

* * *

"Ahhhh, stop it," I shouted out, waking up way too fast. I swatted at Leo, who was licking my face. I sat up and blinked to remember where I was. The room was darker, but not night yet. The gold clock over the fireplace said five thirty.

"Five thirty? Wow, I conked out," I muttered to myself.

The dream I'd been having was still in my head, but cloudy. Something had crawled out of the mine pond and was licking my face with its big nasty tongue. Slobber was everywhere, both in my dream and on my face. I sat up and wiped my wet mouth with my sleeve.

"You got me all slobbery, Leo," I said to him. He didn't care. He just sat there thumping his tail and looking at me with his happy-dog face.

And then more of the dream popped into my head. I remembered Gram being really mad at me for something. She and Uncle Neal had decided to ship me off to someplace in Canada. I could see by Uncle Neal's grin that he was as happy as a clam about it. He leaned over and told Gram that she could now relax and stop worrying about where I was and why I was always late for dinner. She was looking at me through narrowed-down eyes and nodding, which seemed so strange to me because I'd never ever seen Gram with that kind of angry expression. I figured I'd done something really bad to get her to wear one of Uncle Neal's faces, and agree to kick me out of the country.

Then, in my dream, I'd heard banging around in the kitchen and there was Cletus. He was getting into the cupboard and had his whole hand in a peanut butter jar, scooping out huge gobs to shove in his mouth.

"Cletus, where's Pepper?" I asked him.

"She's in the trunk," he chuckled.

I rushed out of the house to rescue her, but the Plymouth wasn't there. I looked all around, but there was nothing but trees, mountains, and an opening to a mine. I rushed back into the house, but Cletus was gone. He'd left his mess in the kitchen, though. Then I saw my big duffle bag right by the front door. I could see it was packed and ready. Uncle Neal was grinning at me with his arms crossed on his chest. He walked over and handed me a map.

"Canada's a big country, Little Mister. Hope ya don't get lost up there."

And then he burst out laughing.

* * *

I let out a big sigh, glad that it was all just a dream, and then remembered that Pepper might still be locked in Cletus' trunk. Or worse.

I again looked at my watch and it hit me that Gram and Uncle Neal weren't home. I got up and looked at the note Uncle Neal had written. I was getting a little worried. Leo was standing next to me, panting and wagging his tail. "You hungry?" I asked him, and he started jumping in circles. When Leo gets excited, he doesn't just wag his tail, he wags his whole body. He has a hinge in his middle that lets him bend almost in half, which gets his tail whipping in a wide and dangerous arch.

But I was nervous and sad as I stumbled through the kitchen to the laundry room . . . . I kept thinking about the dream. I never really cared if I made Uncle Neal angry because he pretty much always was. In fact, that was

Gram's biggest argument with him; that he was always "grousing" about something. "You're making this house an unpleasant place, Neal," I heard her tell him one time. He certainly made my life unpleasant.

Gram, though, was the opposite. She could find fresh strawberries in a cow pie. Gramps once told me that every wrinkle on Gram's face is connected to her smile. So, seeing her frowning and talking about shipping me off to Canada—even in a dream—got me choked up.

Somehow, all this dream stuff had tried to worm its way into what I really needed to be thinking about . . . how to rescue Pepper. I needed to get back on track. While I was thinking about all that, I got out Leo's food. He was still jumping circles in the laundry room; smacking me, then the washer. Then he knocked over the garbage can, which hit a broom, which knocked down the pegboard that held all the keys. Rings and fobs and twenty keys went everywhere.

"Leo, you wild man." I started picking up the mess and was suddenly holding the key to Gramps' Dodge pickup. I just stared at it for a few seconds. It was silver and worn smooth from a thousand times his fingers had started that old truck. Its teeth were mostly gone and I doubted I could even get it to work. Gramps always had to hold it just right to get it to turn, and then he'd say he needed to get a new one made, someday. A lot of things rushed into my head with that key. That's when the idea hit me. And that's when the phone started ringing.

I grabbed it. "Hello?" My heart was beating fast with my new idea.

"Why're you shouting, Calvin?" Uncle Neal said.

"Ah, I dunno . . . running around, I guess."

"Well, knock it off. You'll break something."

"Yes, I won't break anything. Are you coming home?"

"We're not. Not till tomorrow," he said. "The doctor wants to do a few more tests, so we're staying overnight with Aunt Gerty in Bingen."

"Is Gram okay?" I was already worried about Pepper and now Gram was sick.

"She's fine, Calvin. Don't make something out a nothing," he said, trying to sound cheerful. But sounding cheerful is not in Uncle Neal's box of moods.

"Well, what kind of tests?" I wanted to know because when Gramps was ill, everyone tried to pretend that he was fine and wouldn't tell me anything. I knew, though, that something was wrong. He started not wanting to get up early or take me with him. And then he stopped wanting to go anywhere. Gram had quiet conversations with people, and when I came in the room everyone looked at me and smiled, and wanted to talk about my model airplanes or what books I was reading. All I wanted to know was what was going on with my Grandpa.

"Calvin, it's none of your business," Uncle Neal snapped over the phone.

"It is too," I yelled back. "It is too my business!"

Uncle Neal went quiet. I'd never talked back to him. I'd never talked back to anyone before. He didn't say anything, but I heard some scuffling around and murmur talking, and then Gram came on the line.

"Calvin, honey, I'm fine. I've just been feeling a little under the weather is all. Now, I fixed you tuna, so make yourself a sandwich. And guess what?"

"What?" I was interested, but still worried about her. Her voice dropped down to a whisper.

"There's a bag of barbecue chips out in the garage. That old stinker, Uncle Neal, bought them for himself, but you go get 'em." She knew I loved BBQ chips on my tuna sandwiches.

"Now, you listen up," she continued. "Next to your Grandpa, you're the best thing that's ever happened to me and I'm gonna be around a long time to make sure you know that someone always loves you."

I laughed and she chuckled. "I'll be home tomorrow, and we'll get us some Rocky Road and watch Lucy together," she said in her smiling voice. I knew she was smiling . . . Gram smiled all the time. She even smiled at funerals. She'd be so busy comforting everyone else and telling them what a great person so 'n so was that she almost forgot to be sad. I could tell, though, that Gram was also putting a smile on what was really going on.

I decided to wait until she got home to try and wedge it out of her. She gave me Aunt Gerty's number and we hung up.

That conversation reminded me that she'd been a little slower and resting more, lately. Even though she tried to never let me see her that way, I had. I was just in a hurry all the time and it hadn't sunk in.

As I stared at the Dodge key laying on the counter in front of me, I decided I couldn't do it; I just couldn't let Gram down by running off and getting into trouble again. She always lets me off the hook, even when I probably should be left to hang there for a few days. I was about to put the key back when James knocked on the door and let himself in.

"Hey, weren't you gonna wake me?" He looked sleepy with straw in his messed up hair, then looked at me. "What's the matter?"

"Well, nothing, I hope. Gram and Uncle Neal are still in White Salmon. Her doctor wants to do some more testing, but she won't tell me what for."

My finger was spinning the Dodge key on the counter as I talked. James noticed it.

"Is that the key to yer Gramps' truck?"

I stopped spinning it and went to go hang it back on the hook.

"Does it even run anymore?" he asked. He followed me into the laundry room.

"I dunno."

"We could see."

The same idea I'd had was now in his head.

"We could," I said, not meaning it.

"We could take it," James said.

"I don't even know if it runs anymore," I said.

"Well, let's go find out," he said, sounding impatient.

"I was going to, then, when Gram just called . . . I don't want to disappoint her." I looked at him, trying to make him see how important Gram was to me. He knew. And he knew I hated to upset her. Right now, though, I don't think he cared.

He blew out a big breath.

"Well, I'll tell ya who's gonna be disappointed . . . my little sister when she finds out we had a truck and didn't use it. Cal, we're not stealing it or anything. We need to go rescue Pepper, and there's a perfectly good truck sitting up there behind the barn."

"But what about Gram?"

"What about her? They're in White Salmon. We're gonna go nab Pepper and be back home before midnight," he said, as if his sister was sitting on the Carter's front porch waiting for us to pick her up. That wasn't true, so bragging that we'd be home by midnight was ridiculous. Nevertheless, James has his effect on me and, right then, he was starting to make sense.

"Can we do that?" I asked. "Nab her and be home before midnight?"

"I dunno for sure. Maybe twelve-fifteen," he said and then smiled and slugged me on the shoulder. He snatched the key and opened the door.

"Come on, Cal, time to put on our Superman suits."

I looked at him closely. Here I was again with my toe on the line and not wanting to step over, while James was already on his way.

We hurried to the barn.

"What's wrong with Gram?" he asked again.

"It's something she doesn't want to tell me about, which probably means it's something bad."

My eyes welled up, but I quickly wiped them with my sleeve.

Chapter 8

THE OLD RATTLETRAP

There it sat, forgotten behind the barn—Gramps' 1953 Dodge truck. Uncle Neal had driven it one time, right after he'd come to live with us. He complained the whole way to the feed store and back, swearing he'd never drive that "old rattle trap" again.

Well, that was just fine with me. I loved that truck and hoped I could have it when I started driving. Gramps had told me I could, but I doubted Uncle Neal would stick to that promise.

"Probably gonna need some gas," James said.

"There's a can in the barn somewhere, for the mower," I said and pointed. While James went to find the gas, I climbed in behind the wheel. Instantly, the smells hit me in the face. Musty seat covers. The stained bag of tobacco for wiping off the foggy windshield sat where Gramps had left it, right there, handy on the dash. The smells made my eyes water again, thinking about Gramps and all the fun we'd had in this truck.

I stuck in the key and turned it on. The gauges suddenly glowed. "Battery's still good," I said to myself. The gas pedal was squeaky as I pumped it a bunch of times and pulled the choke. I was trying to copy what I'd watched Gramps do a hundred times. The starter button was on the floor and I had to stretch to reach it. The old engine growled and moaned as it turned over. It sounded grumpy about it. I guess I'd woken it from a deep sleep, which in a way I guess we had. The battery was low, so I stopped cranking it.

James appeared with the gas can. "Hold on," he said.

"Let me prime the carburetor." I pulled the hood latch and it popped. He held up a can of starter fluid and after one shot of that ether, the old Dodge started right up. He grinned and gently closed the hood. He sliced across his throat for me to shut it off, which I did.

After emptying the gas can into the tank, we crept the truck down the little two-track road behind Gram's place to Old Bridge Road. It wasn't dark yet, but the road went through the trees. Which is why no one saw us leave. It's probably too bad . . . might have saved us a pile of trouble.

Chapter 9

A LONG LINE OF EVIL

Everybody knew Gramps' truck, so anyone seeing us driving it would have wondered what was going on. We snaked our way down a few irrigation roads and along the outskirts of town until we were finally out into the country. Not too long after that, we were into the woods. But all that messing around cost us time and gas, and put us in the wrong direction to the Carters. At one point James had me pull into a ranch where he knew no one was home and we rooted around for more gas.

The whole time, we kicked around ideas for a plan. We knew why Cletus had come back to the mine, but it was what he was doing now that had us talking in circles; now his plan had derailed and he'd kidnapped Pepper.

"He's gotta be scared Derrick'll find out he was up there," I said. "And he knows we know the score."

"I remember hearing Derrick say that this was his deal and his momma didn't know about it," James said.

"How's he gonna explain a kidnapped little girl?" I added. That shut us both up for a few minutes. Then I asked another question, "What if Pepper's not there?" I instantly wished I hadn't asked because I saw James' jaw tighten.

"Dunno, Cal," he said with more *James* in his voice. "We're gonna find that big pig, Cletus, and get it out of him." He looked back at me and I could see he was serious.

"Maybe they kidnap people all the time," he added. "And then get the ransom money. They're not gonna get much from my mom . . . we've got nothing."

Every way we turned this over, we couldn't figure out

what was next. We finally stopped talking and I just drove and James gave me directions.

* * *

I knew a little bit about the Carters from one time when me and Gramps were filling my bike tires at the gas station. We'd seen Derrick's dad, Darvin Carter, having an argument with Mr. King, the old man who runs the station. Darvin had grabbed Mr. King and pulled him up close and was snarling something about his bill. Two little Carter kids were there and one of them kicked Mr. King in the shin.

"Hey, you little squirt!" Mr. King had hollered, but the kid just laughed and kicked him again. Darvin Carter ignored his brat and kept shaking and yelling at Mr. King. Gramps had stood up and I could see that he was concerned.

"Darvin," Gramps said in a loud voice, "ease up, there! You can get it worked out without tearing Mel's shirt."

Darvin glared over at Gramps and let go, but before he did, he gave Mr. King a little shove and the old man stumbled backwards. Things settled down and the men went in the office to fix whatever needed fixing.

Gramps went back to airing my tires, but he kept an eye on the office window, trying to pretend he wasn't. "That's Darvin Carter. You steer wide around those Carters, you hear me, Calvin?"

"Darvin's heading off to prison, if he doesn't slip out of the state first," Gramps explained on the way home. "He hurt a man real bad down at the mill in Bingen. He's sayin' it was self-defense, but Darvin's a hot head and no one's believin' his story." He looked at me. I could see he was serious. Normally Gramps' mouth had a permanent smile, but right then, it was shoved over to the side.

"People get on a wrong path and it can be hard to get off," he continued, now sounding a little sad. "That's been Darvin's story for years. Fightin' and stealin' and generally causing trouble his whole life. The judge sent him to reform school when he was a kid, but the seeds were sowed and he was in trouble all the time after that."

Gramps sat there quiet as he drove. When we reached the house and stopped, he looked me in the eyes.

"Calvin, you're a good, good boy. You need to just watch yourself and remember who's watching your back, and you'll be alright."

He pointed up and winked, then rubbed the top of my head and grinned.

* * *

It was dark by the time James said, "Okay, now we're lookin' for a little two-track." While he was peering hard out the windows of the Dodge, he brought up the subject of the treasure.

"There's a lot a coins in that chest," he said, low and mysterious.

"James, I think we should get Pepper and forget the coins." He wasn't listening.

"Not far now," he said, pointing at a rundown campground. "I'd bet a year's school lunch that money is stolen."

Well, duh, I thought, but didn't say it out loud.

"What would you do with that many coins?" he asked.

Neither of us had any real idea of how many coins were in the little chest. A mess, I figured. It had been all we could do to lift the dang thing.

"Well, I'd probably help Gram," I said. "And my dad."

"Me too, that's what I'd do too . . . I'd help my mom," he said, very serious.

I knew what he was trying to say. He wanted me to see that he wasn't going to spend it on a boat or a car, which he wanted real bad. I understood. I just knew there were a lot of strings tied to that chest of coins.

James didn't look at me, but kept searching for the Carter's road.

Chapter 10

BEWARE OF JUNKYARD DOGS

"How much further?" I asked. We'd gone another couple miles, and driving slow too, looking for the Carter's road. James hadn't exaggerated when he said the Carters "lived a ways" out from town. It's so far into the hills, you could say they don't actually live in Mud Lake. From what Gramps and James had said, it's a good thing too. If they lived any closer, either a war would break out or everyone would leave and they'd have Mud Lake to themselves.

"It's gotta be close," James muttered, almost to himself. "Slow down some more. We gotta be careful when we get there."

Then he looked at me for a second. "Ya know, I heard Sheriff Stubbs won't even come up here by himself." His hushed tone made the Carter place sound haunted or something. The light from the dashboard gave his face a very spooky look too.

"James, is this a good idea? Coming up here by ourselves, I mean."

"Who we gonna call? Sheriff Stubbs?"

I didn't answer. I didn't have any good ideas, so I figured it was just us.

We finally saw the Carter's little road. It was so overgrown that I guessed they'd planted scrappy maples and little pines to hide it from people hurrying by. If we hadn't been looking, we would have missed it. Now I was driving really slow, mainly because the two-track lane that led down to their house was all rutted and full of holes.

"Cut the lights, Cal."

We drove a little further, then suddenly James pointed. "Up there. See 'em?" he said. The Carter's house lights flicked on and off as trees crossed our view. "Let's hide the truck and hoof-it in."

We spied a little cut into the forest and wormed the truck into a good hiding place. I started to open my door and remembered how the bent door always complained. I followed James out his door.

The house was further than it looked. Especially since we were walking through the woods, slow and sneaky. We didn't have lights, so we both tripped a few times, which made us walk even slower. The night forest has its own special sounds. An owl hooted and was answered by another one deeper in the forest. Their quick and mournful hoots echoed in the trees. It just makes the woods at night creepy. Something scurried across our path, chased by something else. We pulled up and let them pass.

"What if there's someone outside, kind of guarding or watching for us?" I whispered. "What if they have dogs?"

"We'll see them before they see us," James whispered back.

Maybe. Or maybe not, I thought.

When we reached the edge of the woods and could really see the house, it was all lit up. You'd think they were having a birthday party or something. The light spilled out and helped us see a little bit of the front yard.

"Holy cow-pies," James whispered. "Look at all the junk."

Well, there wasn't really a front yard; the Carters had a junkyard. No grass, that I could see, just dirt and more stuff than I could take in. Washers and dryers. A freezer with its door hanging open. Several dead animals—wrapped in blood-stained cloth—were hanging from a tree limb. Two tattered couches and an old chair with its stuffing poking out sat by a fire pit. Fuel drums, stacks of pallets. A long row of console TVs, every one of them with their "big eye" shot out. But the cars were what stood out the most. Cars on blocks. A row of cars with "for sale" signs in the windshields. A couple trucks lying on their sides, and a station wagon upside down. That was strange, in a yard full of strange things.

"Looks like Martians must a dumped all their outer-space trash," James whispered. "Come on."

We didn't see anyone outside, and there was no barking, so we crouched down and took off running at a slow trot. If we'd been playing army, this would've been the best place ever. There were so many things to hide behind and dodge between, we could have played out here for a month and never hidden behind the same things twice.

We made it to an old Pontiac and had a good view of what was going on inside. None of the windows had drapes, so the lights from the house made angled squares on the ground and the junk. We could see at least three men in the front room watching a snowy TV . . . and a couple of big dogs on a ratty couch . . . conked out . . . thank you, God . . .

And then we spotted Pepper, parked in a chair, listening to someone we couldn't see. A big hairy man was behind her with his hands on her shoulders. Another man came in the room and stopped near her. Then, the biggest, meanest looking lady I'd ever seen walked into view and bent down in Pepper's face. From the backside, her dress resembled a flowery tent. She turned and faced toward the window and I saw how her hair was piled up on top of her head like a huge scoop of hairy ice cream.

"That's Carmelita," James whispered. "Her kids call her Momma."

Whatever Carmelita was saying, Pepper wasn't giving her the answers she wanted. Carmelita's head wagged from side to side and her mouth was going a mile a minute. She then looked and waved to someone we couldn't see. The big hairy man jerked Pepper's head back and got down close. He wasn't happy about her answers either and yelled at someone so loud we could hear him. "Cletus. Get yer sorry . . ." That's all we heard, but then Cletus appeared from another room. Maybe the kitchen, because he was eating a chicken leg.

There he was, still in his ratty jeans and grimy tee shirt. In the light, I could see that his hair was long and stringy and thick with grease. He was hunched over and looked either sad or scared . . . I couldn't tell.

"He looks like he has a load of bricks on his shoulders," I whispered.

Carmelita, the hairy man, and Cletus were arguing about what Pepper must have said. Cletus kept pointing at her and shaking his head and finger, and Carmelita and the hairy man kept looking at Pepper and asking questions. Pepper would then shake her head and say things back at Cletus that didn't look very nice.

"I wonder where Derrick is?" James asked. "I hope Pepper's sticking to her story."

"Whatever that is," I muttered.

Suddenly, Pepper leaned forward and shouted something at Carmelita. And the big lady slapped her. The man behind Pepper had to grab the chair so it wouldn't tip over. Everyone else in the room watched as Carmelita said something else to Pepper and Pepper kicked her in the shin. She staggered sideways and her hand went up, ready for another slap.

"We gotta do something, Cal." James was mad . . . and maybe a little desperate.

Instead of hitting Pepper, Carmelita said something harsh to the hairy man. He grabbed Pepper and hauled her out of the room. A big discussion broke out, with some finger pointing at Cletus. I suddenly felt helpless. We were just two kids, and the Carters had a house full of grown men. We sure weren't going to "storm the beaches," which was what Gramps sometimes said when he wanted to get something hard done fast.

"We need to get everyone to run out of the house," I said, and started looking around the yard. "Create some kind of distraction."

"Right," James whispered. "A distraction so we can rush in and grab her!" His head instantly swirled back and forth as he also searched the yard for an opportunity. Both of our brains were working in high gear.

"I don't really see anything," I said. "Maybe there's something in the backyard."

The back of the house was the same as the front—junk, junk, and more junk. And more cars and some big trucks. We hand-signaled to split up and started looking for anything that might make noise. The backyard was darker because only one window had a light on. Probably the kitchen, I thought. It was right next to the backdoor. I tripped on a garden hose and thought, maybe I can flood the place. As I was following it along the ground I started to smell gas, and then almost ran into a big rusty propane tank. It looked like a giant hotdog.

"This thing is leaking," I whispered to myself. I wiggled the copper hose that went into the ground and it was loose. I yanked on it and it pulled up from the dirt.

"Shouldn't this be deeper in the ground?" I muttered in amazement. I stood and looked at it and then looked at the house. "I could blow the whole house up. Or, just make it stink like it's gonna blow up."

I looked around and saw James bobbing in and out of the cars. "James," I shouted in my loudest whisper. I could just barely make out his silhouette in the darkness. He turned just as the backdoor opened and someone came out. I ducked down behind the propane tank. It was Cletus, hustling over to an outhouse. But then someone else came out.

"Hey Cleets, wait up," the man yelled.

Cletus stopped right near the propane tank I was

crouched behind. Too close for my liking. Plus, I was getting a face full of stinky gas. I hoped I didn't throw up.

"Let's talk turkey," the second guy said. "What were you doin' up there, anyway?"

"Scoutin' for sheds," Cletus said.

"You gettin' the jump on the rest of us?"

"Shudup, Mikey," Cletus interrupted.

I peeked out and saw that the guy named Mikey was the one who'd been standing behind Pepper. He laughed. But it wasn't a fun laugh. It was a dangerous Derrick kind of laugh.

"Take it easy, Cleets," Mikey said. He then lowered his voice and got all secretive. But I was close enough to hear. "Hey, what was you and Dee up to the other day? Eh?"

"Nothin' . . . we was doing a thing for Dee, that's all."

"A thing for Dee? What kind a thing? Can I get in on this thing?" Mikey asked, sounding sneaky. I suddenly figured these Carters were always doing things behind each other's backs.

"Ya have ta ask Dee," Cletus said.

"Can't. He's off somewhere doing another thing," Mikey said. "That's why I'm askin' you, Cleets."

"Have ta talk with Dee about that. I'm just the muscle," Cletus said.

"Ah, so this thing was heavy," Mikey said, sounding like he'd just discovered another clue.

"Talk ta Dee, Mikey. I just was helpin' is all."

Mikey slapped Cletus on the back. "Don't blame ya, Cleets. Momma's been really rough on you, lately. I'd skedaddle too, if it was me. Hit the trail and make my move. Make my own way," Mikey said in a kind of dreamy, adventurous way.

"I ain't skedaddlin' nowhere," Cletus whined. "I got nowhere ta skedaddle to. That little girl's gonna get me some cash. Count on that, man."

"Right. Okie dokie, then," Mikey said. I could almost

hear the sarcasm in his voice. He aimed Cletus toward the outhouse and went back inside. I figured Mikey had been sent out to try and poke holes in Cletus' story. While Cletus was doing his business, James found me.

"What'd you find?" James whispered.

"Take a sniff."

"Propane? You wanna blow up the house?"

"No, not with Pepps inside. But there's a garden hose. We can . . ."

I stopped because Cletus came out and slammed the outhouse door. He slowly shuffled back to the house, but stopped at the door. I could tell by the way he was shifting from one foot to the other that he didn't want to go back inside. I didn't blame him. When he did finally go in, I started to breathe again.

"We'll run the garden hose out and make a distraction out there," I explained and pointed toward the big trucks scattered around the yard. James' face lit up and he nodded.

If this was just us, out in the woods somewhere, and we'd found this tank and hose, well this would be fun. Scary, but fun. Blowing up the Carter's yard, with Pepper inside their house, made me nervous. But, just the word 'boom' always gets James' attention.

I told you about the mine and the dynamite, well there were a few other times when we got a hold of explosives that I'll tell you about some other time.

But right now, we'd found some wire and connected it to a car battery, and broken the propane tube and shoved it into the garden hose, which we'd run out to some of the old trucks.

"Are we ready?" James whispered.

We were sitting as far away as we could and still be able to see what might happen inside the house.

"I'm actually kind of scared, James. This is going to be really noisy."

"That's the point, Cal. Make 'em run like scared cats."

I put my hands over my ears and squinted down my eyes. He closed his and touched the wires.

Chapter 11

THOUGHTS FROM A HOLLOW HEAD

What came next was like a strange dream. Only, more real than a dream, but also not connected very well.

I remember the loudest WOOSH I'd ever heard and my eyelids turned bright red. Then, I heard yelling. And being grabbed and pulled. Something was on fire and when my eyes skimmed past trees, they were glowing red. Smoke blew in my face, then cleared. I felt myself being roughly dragged and rolled into a truck's bed. More yelling. A loud, hateful woman giving orders.

My eyes fluttered and opened. I thought I was looking through a fan, my fast blinking chopped what I saw into snapshots. James was lying on his side. He was looking at me. His face was black and a tiny stream of blood was running down his forehead. Someone was sitting behind him, I saw their jeans. Some rope was near my face. A tire jack. Animal skins. A few traps. I understood we were in the back of a pickup. Then, me and James, and the legs, bounced into the air and landed again. We'd hit a big bump. I could see James make a face.

"I'm hungry," someone said. Cletus, maybe.

"Well, tough. We ain't stoppin'. That's for sure," another voice said. I think it was that Mikey guy, who'd come out to question Cletus.

"I never seen Auntie Carma so mad," Cletus said.

"She was a mess a hornets, for sure," Mikey agreed.

The legs shifted, and big hands rolled James a little to look in his face. "This one's awake," Mikey said. "You wanna tell us why you blew up our house?" James just moaned and Mikey let his head drop back to the truck bed. "Don't matter. Uncle Donte'll find out what's going on whidd these two."

When my eyes opened again, the sky was pink. James was sitting up, but slumped over and his eyes were closed. We were still in the truck, but on pavement, I guessed. I tried to move my hands and feet but they were tied up tight.

"You ain't goin' nowhere," the first voice said and his foot gave me a shove. "Well, that ain't exactly the truth."

I couldn't focus my eyes or brain. Have you ever had someone show you their box of old family photos? They pull out photos and then say to you, "this is my uncle on his farm" or "this girl is my cousin from Idaho" or "that's my old dog, Skipper." To you, the pictures aren't really connected. Well, that's what this was like. Every time I woke up—which wasn't really awake—it was like the box of pictures. The guy's boots. Then some clouds. James' face. Heads—with mussed up hair—bouncing in the cab of the truck. Then I noticed the trees as they blurred past the sky. The pines and fir trees had turned to oaks. We weren't in Mud Lake anymore.

I tried to ask a question, but my brain and mouth were somehow disconnected. Mikey and the other guy laughed at whatever I was attempting to say.

"Take the marshmallows outta yer mouth, Junior Mint," Mikey laughed. My lips felt fat and flabby and I tasted blood. I realized I must have been hit with something. Even though I'm telling you the things I saw and heard, they were blurry bits and pieces. A lot like a mirror I once broke. It somehow stayed in the frame, but its reflection was all splintered and shattered into funny strips.

I saw and heard other things, but I can't seem to get a hold of them to tell you. That's why I knew I must have been hit on the head with something when everything blew up.

When I finally was able to sneak a look over at James, I thought he was out. His head lulled from side to side, but then his eye peeked open and winked at me. He was faking it. That's when I knew he was probably looking forward to what was next. I wasn't. I was scared.

I think you already know that being best friends with James is risky business. About half the time we just have fun and nothing really bad happens. The other half, however, one of us gets hurt, which is usually me. James seems to actually look for that kind of danger, and him winking at me, right after we'd just blown up the Carter's backyard, and maybe their house, and them all wanting to tear our arms off, told me that he was somehow enjoying this scary ride.

Blowing up anybody's house would make them madder than a rattlesnake; blowing up the Carter's house, well, even though I wasn't thinking clearly, I was still able to imagine things they would do to us.

I closed my eyes and tried to connect the random dots and reassemble what had happened. We had stuck a broken propane tube into the garden hose. Cletus was talking to someone. James had run off for something. I disconnected the hose from the house. He came back with a car battery. But that's about it. Somehow we'd done it . . . we'd created a distraction, but blown ourselves into captivity instead.

Pepper came into focus in my mind. Then I saw the hairy guy drag her from view. That's why we were there, to get Pepper. Where is Pepper?

I don't remember stopping. But, I did get a big whiff of a river's wet, muddy smell. It must be the Columbia. Something woody was there too. Sawdust, I decided.

Maybe we're around Bingen, I thought.

I tried to push myself up and someone yanked me into a sitting position and blindfolded me with a handkerchief. The few seconds before, though, confirmed we were at the Columbia River and near Bingen, at least thirty miles from home.

Gramps had worked in Bingen after the Mud Lake Mill shut down. Every day he made the long drive and did the same job he'd done in Mud Lake mill; he ran a saw. Bingen was mainly a mill, parked on the bank of the Columbia River. White Salmon was up the hill, and that's where everybody got their supplies.

"You punks are at the end of the line," Mikey said. I heard car doors closing. Then I heard them dragging James.

"He's still out," someone said.

"Then carry 'im, ya knucklehead!" A woman bossed him. Carmelita, I guessed.

Then someone grabbed me and hauled me out of the truck and stood me up. But my feet were asleep and I almost tipped over. Hands roughly aimed me and started walking me forward. We stepped onto bouncy wood planks. Gangway, I thought. I knew the feeling from being around the river in Portland. Then my feet found a dock and the hands shoved and guided me forward. Through a door and into the strong smell of a musty old room. Pushed down onto a couch. I sank into its crummy cushions. My blindfold was jerked off my face and I blinked at the people in the room.

Carmelita was the one who'd pulled it off and she stood in front of me, blocking most of my view. I looked up at her and she sneered down at me.

"Well, aren't you just adorable," she said and snorted a laugh. I just blinked. I was sure I wasn't adorable. Nobody but Gram had ever called me adorable. "You won't think yer so cute when I get you up ta Pasco," she added.

Pasco?

Then someone pulled me off the couch and shoved me down at the table. Carmelita leaned down, acting real chummy. She was smoking and blew a gray cloud into my face.

Up close, Carmelita was awful. Her skin was yellow and

full of strange dents. I wondered if maybe a shotgun had gone off in her face when she was a kid. Also, I smelled bad meat and sweat. It was Carmelita I was smelling. I think my nose must have scrunched up because a she sneered at me. I think she was trying to smile, but it just gave me the heebie-jeebies.

"Yes sir, Pasco's where the fun starts, Little Fella," she said. "You're gonna give my brother, Donte, something to work on for . . . oh, maybe a couple days," she said. "And then, well, I ain't really sure. There might not be much left after . . ."

She cackled and stepped back. I could now see the whole room with its trashy, worn out furniture. A couch and chairs with torn fabric. Plates with dried food sitting on a three-legged coffee table, its missing leg propped up with an ammunition box.

I saw Pepper in a corner. She was still blindfolded and turning her head around trying to see out the bottom. It was dull light because all the windows were covered with stained bed sheets and held up with clothes pins. The carpet had big dark blotches and the whole place smelled of mold and fish. I knew we were on a houseboat . . . I could feel it slowly rocking.

A mismatched set would be how I'd describe the Carters. I would have had a hard time picking out brothers from cousins because their close-set eyes and downturned mouths were so similar. All their hairlines rode low across their foreheads and scowling eyebrows shaded their dark eyes. Also, everyone's ears swung wide from their scalps. They reminded me of open car doors or tiny wings. If there'd been enough wind, they'd probably flap.

Everyone but Carmelita lounged around like lazy bears, with their legs draped over chair arms or stuck straight out into the middle of the room. They just watched with sleepy eyes while Carmelita was roughing us up. We were obviously the only entertainment.

Mikey pulled me from the table and threw me down on a couch where I crashed into James.

"Get this off my face," James mumbled and thrashed his head from side to side. Even though our hands were still tied, he found my shoulder and tried to push the handkerchief off. But Mikey pulled him away and forcibly took him to the table, where Carmelita removed the blindfold.

James looked around the room, then up at Carmelita. He was blinking, trying to get his eyes to work.

"Where are we?" he demanded.

"You're with me now, Bub," Carmelita spat back at him while stabbing her finger into his face.

"When the cops find you . . ." James didn't get to finish because she slapped him and he toppled off the chair. He sprang back up though, just like a Tommy Tippy Cup I'd had as a kid. Then Mikey grabbed James from behind and tossed him back on the couch, his head landing hard against my shoulder.

"No more of that nonsense outta either a you punks," she snarled with her gravelly smoker's voice.

The door suddenly swung open and a man with a good haircut and glasses came in. He stopped in the open door, looked at me and James, and then scanned the room. Carmelita put her hands on her hips and snapped at him, "Well, look who's late to the party."

He didn't say anything. He was scowling and looking from Carmelita to us and back at her.

"What's all this?"

He was dressed up and wearing a tie, but I could tell he was a Carter. Just a clean version of one.

"Some unexpected visitors," Carmelita said, lighting a cigarette. "Need you ta check 'em out, Floyd, and then we gotta go . . ."

He must be a doctor, I thought. Someone dragged over a chair and he sat down in front of me and James.

"So, what's the story with these two? And all these

burns? What happened, Carmelita?"

"They blew up my backyard and my house!"

Doctor Floyd didn't even flinch, he just pulled out a penlight and aimed it into my eyes.

I wondered if he'd come down to the houseboat just to see me and James. He was a Carter alright. He'd just gone through the wash or something, unlike the rest of Carmelita's grubby brood. He was even wearing aftershave.

I blinked from his light.

"Hold your eyes open for a second." He watched closely and his eyebrows went up, kind of like Uncle Neal's when he didn't believe me. I would never have thought I'd miss Uncle Neal, but right then, I did.

"Hmmm, this one has a mild concussion," he said low and thoughtful. "He should be in the hospital, I'd say." He then touched my swollen lips and a place on my head that was sore. "You have some ice? We need to cool off these hot spots."

"Get some ice," Carmelita barked to everyone in the room. She tapped the doctor on the shoulder. "No one here's goin' to any hospital, Floyd. You need to get these two straightened around for some travel."

"I ain't goin' to Pasco," Pepper suddenly shouted out. No one paid any attention, except for Mikey who walked over and gave her a little shove.

"Hey," she snapped.

"Leave her alone," James yelled out at Mikey and tried to get up, but whoever was behind us jammed him back onto the couch.

"Keep yer seat till the ride's over," said the man. All the Carter boys chuckled.

Doctor Floyd looked around at everyone, but didn't say anything. He scooted his chair over to James and lifted his head. He frowned as he did it and looked through his glasses funny, as if the lower part of the lenses were better than the top.

"This one could also use better care than I can give him down here," he muttered. He touched James' head where he had been bleeding. The ice arrived and the doctor put it on the swollen lump on James' head. James winced.

"Where else you hurting?" Doctor Floyd asked us.

"Nowhere," James spat out. "Let us go." He again tried to get up, but was pushed back down.

"No sir, young man," Carmelita said. She was serious and leaned in close, over the doctor's shoulder. "You blew up my place. Someone could a got killed. Now, you get to come with us."

She jabbed one of her cigarette-stained fingers into James' chest. He just glared back at her. It suddenly occurred to me that Carmelita and her bunch might have their hands full with James. I knew I wasn't going to be any trouble, and I didn't think Pepper would be either. James, though, wasn't going to put up with her poking him for long.

Doctor Floyd casually pushed Carmelita's hand out of his way and went back to looking James over.

I noticed Cletus standing back in the shadows. He looked very nervous and was chewing his nails and watching all the activity. I'm sure he hoped Carmelita and the others were done asking him questions.

"Get the boat ready," Carmelita barked over her shoulder. "We'll shove off as soon as Cousin Floyd's done with these two mutts."

Cletus came to life and followed another Carter out the door. Doctor Floyd got up and walked Carmelita into another room. As they were leaving, he said to anyone in the room, "Get these three some water and something to eat."

He also popped open his little leather doctor bag and pulled out a bottle of pills. "Give the two boys one of these." He shook out pills into his hand and handed them to Mikey.

James gave me a quick elbow. I instantly knew it meant

something, but what? My mind started running down a list: Run for it? Grab something for a weapon? Fake sleeping? Don't take the pills? It hit me . . . don't take the pills.

"What are they?" James demanded.

"Something to . . ." Doctor Floyd was interrupted by Carmelita.

"You take what he gives you . . . he's a doctor." She snorted a funny laugh. But not funny. I think you know what I mean.

Mikey gave us the pills but I tucked mine under my tongue. When no one was looking I dribbled it out into my lap and closed my legs.

Someone made a mess of sandwiches and everyone, including us, got one. It hurt to eat. In fact, the longer we sat there, the more I felt places that hurt. That blast must have knocked me and James into next week. I had a low ringing in my ears and there were red spots on my arms that must be burns. I took a better look at James. His face was blotchy too, so that must be what I looked like.

In the other room I could hear Carmelita and Doctor Floyd going at it in low voices.

"Not my first circus, Floyd."

"Well, you're playing with something . . ."

"I think you need to mind your own business."

"You've made it my business, Aunt Carmelita."

Every now and then one of them would peek out at us. Carmelita did not look happy.

While they were arguing, the others in the room just ignored them. One of the Carters had turned on a TV to some morning show where everyone was laughing and talking. A guy in a sparkly tux was showing how his dog—also wearing a tux—could dance the Cha-Cha. Gram only watched one daytime TV show, *Peyton Place*, which I thought was boring. Everyone just talked all the time and cried about everything, and someone was always worried about "the baby." I thought *Dr. Kildare* was more interesting, but she said shows about doctors and hospitals made her think of Gramps and so we stopped watching that one.

While everyone was fixated on the dancing dog, I snuck a few looks at James. We both knew we had to come up with a plan or we'd end up in Pasco. I'd heard of Pasco, but didn't know where it was, let alone know what was going to happen when we got there. But they were getting a boat ready, which meant it was near the river and we were going soon.

If we could get to the police—which I'd wanted to do in the first place—we could maybe wiggle ourselves out of this mess. I was sure of one thing; this wasn't going to be a pleasure cruise.

Chapter 12

NIGHT CRUISE ON THE COLUMBIA

I love boats. Well, I guess I should say that I learned to love boats. When I was around six, Dad built a sailboat in the garage and then we spent almost every weekend out on the river. At first I was terrified, but after a while it was fun.

The Carter's boat was an old cabin cruiser, and I mean a real tub. My dad and his sailing pals would've called it "a big ol' floatin' pig."

Just before Doctor Floyd left, he checked on us again. He and Carmelita had a few more spicy words, but he lost that argument. Carmelita's thugs then manhandled the three of us through a door and into the boat garage.

The first thing James said when they shoved us through the door was, "A garage for a boat?" But he was told to shut up and had to just gawk around.

I wasn't kidding about the Carter's boat being a tub. Actually, it was a wreck. It was probably nice a long time ago, but now it needed everything: paint, varnish for the natural woods, and the brass was all green. When we were shoved down the tiny stairs into the main cabin, it was worse. There was more junk than room to sit. Ammunition cases, shoddy old lifejackets, and fishing gear were stacked on one of the seats; and there was a pile of crab pots in the navigation station. It stank of gas and mold.

"Pee-U," said Pepper, as we were being marched through the main cabin, tripping over things as we were forced to hurry into the forward berth. The door slammed behind us and we were finally alone. It still stank up there, just mostly musty. Pepper wrinkled up her nose.

"Stinks in here," she said. I reached over and opened one of the portholes and she stuck her face up to it.

While we were being shoved toward the boat, James had whispered to Pepper to keep her mouth shut and to stop making Carmelita mad. She'd tried to kick her again and kept screaming that she wanted to go home. All her arguing and trouble just made the big lady mad and laugh. How someone could be mad and laugh at the same time was new to me. She reminded me of Derrick when he was laughing at Cletus in the mine . . . evil and cruel.

The forward cabin on any boat is tiny. This one had two bunks that formed a V at the front. The little portholes were only big enough to stick your arm through, but they helped clear out the stink.

I noticed right off that the cabin had a hatch in the ceiling. I tapped James and pointed up. He immediately reached up to open it, but I grabbed his arm.

"No, let them get underway," I whispered. "Once things settle down, we can see if we can use it."

The cruiser was around forty feet long, which is big enough for people to spread out a little. That got me hoping that maybe one of us could escape out the hatch, when everyone was asleep. Probably not all three of us, we'd never have that much time. Unless, maybe at night.

I suddenly pictured a sailing movie I'd seen where pirates were slipping over the deck to attack a ship. I saw us doing that, only escaping. I whispered that to James and Pepper and that started us planning.

"I just hope no one is sitting at the bow," I said. That's where I like to sit, up at the bow to get the spray in my face and feel the boat smash into the waves. I again glanced up at the hatch. It might work, I thought.

While they backed the boat out of the garage, we watched through the portholes. I thought about waving something out the porthole but the houseboat was at the very end of the marina, off by itself, so I doubted anyone was watching us leave.

"Where's Pasco?" I asked James.

"Way up the river. Over a hundred miles, I think."

Pepper started to sob. "We're never gonna see Mom again."

"Yes we will, Pepps. Me and Cal are gonna think of something. You'll see," he whispered. He kept looking out the window though, and his confidence didn't really help because she started to cry.

I can't really tell you why I did this, maybe because Gram has done it to me, but I put my arm around Pepper's shoulder. I knew right off that it was a bad idea because she squished herself into me and wouldn't let go. I looked at James and he looked at me. Both of our eyes were wide and Pepper calmed down. I could see that James was gearing up for a verse of "Cal & Pepper sittin' in a tree," so I shot him my best stink eye and he snorted out a laugh.

The engines roared up and I looked out the porthole. The driver aimed the cruiser to cross the river and after about fifteen minutes the boat was hugging the Oregon shore. Every twenty minutes or so it had to swing out and around the jetties, and then it would come back in close to shore where the current was easy.

"They can't make it to Pasco in one day, I'd guess," James said.

"Yeah, they're going to need gas at some point."

James nodded and looked out a porthole.

"Well, I know what I need," Pepper said, "a bathroom."

"Me too," I said.

James smacked his fist against the door and Mikey jerked it open.

"What?"

"We need to pee," James snapped back.

Mikey nodded and Pepper jumped up first, the door slammed behind her. While she was gone, James and I tried to figure a plan, but all we could come up with was one of us jumping overboard whenever we could get away with it. Then we heard some scuffling, and Pepper complaining. James grabbed the door, but it was locked.

"Hey," he yelled, but no one answered.

I smashed my ear against the door and heard talking. Then I heard Pepper saying "no" and something I couldn't make out.

"They're questioning her," I whispered. "What's our story?"

"The Magpie's our fort," James said and shrugged. "We go there all the time."

"And we play army and explore and camp up there," I added.

"Yeah, because it's ours," James said in a firm voice. "Pepper just followed us up there last night. But then that Cletus showed up. We don't know why."

We talked this all through in tiny whisper voices. Then the door flew open and Mikey shoved Pepper in. She landed on me.

"You," he ordered, pointing at me.

"Wadda you doin'?" James demanded. Mikey just sneered at James, and motioned for me to follow. Someone had cleared out a spot at the table and Carmelita had claimed it. Up close, she was a huge queen in a moo-moo, slurping a beer and smoking a cigarette. A couple of her boys were slouched around on boxes and the stairs to the deck.

"So, Little Man," she said and quickly blew out a cloud of smoke. The cigarette dangled from her lips and bobbed up and down when she spoke. "Tell us what you were doing up there at that mine." Her head was cocked to one side to keep smoke from drifting into her squinty eyes. She slurped her beer without even taking out the cigarette.

"It's our fort," I said.

She didn't say anything, but just sat there waiting.

"We play army up there and explore," I added. "That's what we do all the time. We explore places."

"On a school night. Yer parents should be ashamed a themselves," she said. One of her boys snickered. "I might have ta call that worthless Sheriff Stubbs about you truants. Come on, what were you three up to?"

"Nothing. Sometimes we skip school," I said, trying to sound tough. She just tilted her head and grinned through the smoke that snaked up past her eyes. Her eyes narrowed down even further and the tip of her Camel glowed as she pulled on it. I sure hope James was listening.

"I never would a pegged you for a school skipper," she said with a nasty smile. Smoke poured from her plump, red lips.

"What about that little girl, Pepper? What's her story?"

"She's a little snoop," I said in the snottiest tone I could come up with. "She just got that bike and now she follows us everywhere." Now I was getting somewhere. I knew I sounded annoyed about that. "Who wants your best friend's little sister tagging along when you're gonna climb down some mine shaft." I instinctively looked around at the other boys in the room, who all laughed and nodded their heads.

Camelita shushed them and looked at me with a serious squint.

"Any idea why Cletus was nosing around up there?"

"The guy who grabbed Pepper?" I asked back. She just squeezed her eyebrows together and nodded. I shook my head, no.

"But he smashed our bikes and took off with Pepper."

"Jus' like that," Carmelita said. "He grabbed Pepper."

"I guess so," I said, shrugging my shoulders. "I don't know what he was thinking. Did you ask him?"

She snorted out a snotty laugh and then started coughing. Her eyes bugged out and her face got red. She waved her hand and Mikey took me back. He then hauled James out to talk with Carmelita.

"What'd you say?" I whispered to Pepper.

"Nothing," she said.

"Wadda ya mean, nothing?" I asked, a bit aggravated. "Did she want to know why you were following us?"

"Yeah. And I told her because you guys always do fun stuff and I want to come with you."

I just nodded. That more or less matched what I'd said. I pressed my ear against the door and tried to hear what was going on.

"What were you guys doing up there?" Pepper asked. I just looked at her and waved my hand to be quiet. She made a snotty face back at me.

What I heard was James giving Carmelita a hard time. The bits and pieces I picked out were the same as what I'd said. Then I heard, "Pepper? Who wants their sister . . ." And then laughter.

James said in a louder voice, "I dunno who he is or why he was up there. But he took my little sister and we came up there to get her back!"

A scuffle erupted, and I heard some "oooffing" sounds.

"I think someone got punched," I whispered. There was some more banging around and shouts and then the door burst open and James was shoved into the cabin. He was holding his stomach.

"Got punched by one of those meatheads out there," he huffed out. Then gasped in some air and leaned back.

"Got nothin' outta me," he cough-laughed. "Name, rank, and serial number."

I looked out the porthole. All I saw was the Oregon highway that followed the river, cars zooming past.

"I can climb out and jump overboard and swim to shore," James said.

"Then what? Try to get a car to stop? For a soggy kid who just crawled out of the river?"

"They'd stop," he argued.

"I think we wait for The Dalles and do it when we're coming into the marina." I suggested.

We looked at each other . . . thinking.

"What if there isn't a marina?" Pepper said, sounding like she was one of the gang.

"There's a marina," I whispered to Pepper and James. "We're gonna slow down sometime. That has to be our chance for one of us to escape."

"Well, it won't be you," James said. He didn't say it to be mean, he just knew that me jumping off this boat into the Columbia River would take everything I had. What I realized, though, is that I *could* do it. This wasn't just getting across the Salmon River so we could see what was on the other side. This was a matter of life and maybe death. Carmelita was mad and I was sure her boys would do about anything she ordered. Something suddenly hit me.

"James," I whispered. "I don't think Carmelita knows about the chest of coins."

Pepper perked up and asked, too loud, "What chest of coins?"

James jabbed his finger in front of her face.

"Pepper, it's time to get a mitt and get in this game," he angrily whispered. "Do you understand?"

"Shut up, James," she snapped back at him.

"Maybe Pepper's the one who goes overboard?" James whispered to me.

"What? No. I can't do that," she said, again too loud.

I looked right at her. "Pepper, being mad isn't helping. You're the one who followed us, remember?"

She scowled back at me.

"Yeah," James said, "so quit being such a pain and help."

She then scowled at James.

"We'll explain the whole thing later," I whispered to her, "when it's not so risky." She seemed to accept that and relaxed.

"At least she's not torturing us for that information," James whispered.

Pepper started to ask, but I pointed my finger at her

and her mouth slammed shut. I got the feeling she
wanted me to put my arm around her again, but I didn't. I
did scoot a little closer, though.

Chapter 13

BOUND AND GAGGED FOR PASCO

James was shaking me.

"Hey, wake up," he said and pointed out the porthole. "We're not going to The Dalles. We're passing right by."

I shook off my sleepy head full of cobwebs and stuck my face out the porthole. The town of The Dalles was slipping past us. Pepper put her cheek against mine so she could see too. I quickly let her have the window. She groaned and looked mad.

"Well, they have to get through the locks," James said.

"Maybe they're closed for the night," I suggested. "Then we'll have to stop somewhere."

"And I'll do it then," he whispered very quietly. "If it's clear, we'll all go. If not, then just me."

It was getting dark so we couldn't really see the shore very well. Then the lights of the dam appeared upriver.

"We're slowing down," I said. We peered out the porthole and could see the Oregon side of the river getting closer. One light on a pole came into view. It was some kind of little park or parking area. The boat started to turn toward the light and then we heard feet stomping around and the splash of the anchor.

"We're spending the night here," I said.

"Perfect," James whispered. There was more stomping around and then the low clunks of something hitting the side of the cruiser. We could only pick out bits and pieces of conversations, nothing that told us anything about the Carter's plans for us, only more laughing and more arguing. Then the door swung open and Derrick stood in the frame looking at us. His small, snake-eyes scanned the three of us and then parked on James.

"Shoulda known it'd be a Nelson," he scoffed and laughed.

"How come you know me?" James asked, not happy about being recognized.

Derrick just scoffed and looked at Pepper. "Who's this? Little sister?"

"None of your beeswax," Pepper said back.

Derrick just laughed. But not a fun laugh, either. It was his nasty *I'm-gonna-think-of-some-way-to-kill-you* laugh. As quick as he was smiling, his face got stern and serious.

"What's the big doin's up at the mine?" he asked. He then looked at me and back at James.

"No big doin's," James said, with a big scoop of wise-guy in his voice. "We were just messin' around up there. Besides, that's our mine. It's our fort."

Cousin Floyd pushed past Derrick and the five of us filled up the tiny room. Derrick looked over Doctor Floyd's shoulder. "The dentist is here to check for cavities," He laughed and left. Dr. Floyd kicked the door closed and sat down. He had his bag with him and snapped it open. "I brought some ointment to help with your burns." He started dabbing it on our faces.

"What's the score here, Doc?" James asked.

"Carters six, Kids zero," he murmured. "How this all happened is immaterial at this point. The fact is, you three have become a problem for my Aunt Carmelita." He was looking through his glasses in that funny way again.

"We didn't do nothin'," James said.

"Hmmm, don't believe that."

"Are you a doctor or a dentist?" I asked.

"Dentist."

"Well . . ." I started to say, but he cut me off.

"Long story, Boy." He dabbed around my mouth so I had to keep my lips closed.

"I'm going to suggest you sit tight until folks settle down

for the night," he said in a very low voice, then glanced at the hatch. "I can assure you, you do not want to make it to Pasco."

He held up a tube of ointment, then placed it back in a small box.

"I'm leaving this with you," he said to me. "Be sure you dab it on every hour to keep those burns covered. And here's some aspirin."

He then scanned the tiny room and shook his head. His eyes finally stopped on me and James. He had a funny look in his eye when he looked down at the little ointment box in my hands. He pointed at the box.

"I changed my mind. I want you to put some more of that on in ten minutes," the doctor added in a very serious voice. "Ten minutes . . . and be sure you read the instructions, so you get it right."

He turned around, walked out, and slammed the door.

James and I looked at each other.

"Why in ten minutes?" I asked. "He just put some on."

"Let me see that," James said.

But as I handed him the box, the door flew open and Derrick filled the frame. His face wore a smirk and his head nodded slightly while he leaned against the door-jam and crossed his arms.

"James Nelson," he said slowly, then looked around at the three of us.

"Ain't you a dang gang a outlaws," he growled. "Blew up the place, I hear." He reached out and grabbed James by the shirt and jerked him to his feet. "Again, what were you clowns doing up at that mine?" he snarled, in a very low voice meant for only us to hear.

"Playing army," James said, but not so cocky this time.

I glanced at Pepper. Her eyes were the size of quarters.

Derrick tilted his head to one side and got even closer to James. "Sunday night? Twenty some miles from town, playing army?"

Derrick shoved James to the bed and grabbed Pepper and hoisted her up. "How 'bout you, Pepper? Maybe you and me better go off by ourselves and have a little chat." He was looking at James when he said that. James suddenly stood up.

"Let her go!"

Derrick sneered at James and stiff-armed him. "And what if I don't?"

"She was just following us," James said. "So let her go." Derrick thought this was funny and just pulled her close.

"Nah, I think she's my ace card," he whispered and smiled. "Now, what were you three doing up there?" As he said it, his hands started squeezing Pepper's arms and she winced. I thought she might scream out, but she kept quiet.

James screwed up his mouth and thought for a few seconds. I could see he was scratching out a story. He lowered his voice to let Derrick in on some big secret.

"We got a stash of things up there. Mostly things we've found . . . and then the Plymouth went by and we decided to follow it."

Derrick's eyes narrowed. He looked to me. Was he nibbling on the bait?

"What kind a stuff?" Derrick asked.

"Sheds, mainly. And fun mining tools. We're gonna cash 'em in," James said. "What was that Cletus guy doin' up there and why'd he nab my little sister?"

I could see that James was trying to turn the tables.

"Dunno what dumb Cletus was doin' up there," Derrick said, and shoved Pepper back onto the bed. He leaned into James' face and put his finger right on his forehead. James slapped it away, but he put it right back and pushed hard on James' head.

"You best shut up about that mine, if you know what's good for you," Derrick added. He shot a quick glance at me and Pepper, then noticed the ointment box.

"What's that?" he demanded and reached out his hand.

"Ointment Doctor Floyd gave us," I said and handed it to him. He popped it open and dumped out the little tube and glanced at it. He tossed it back on the bed and left. We all let out a sigh and looked at each other. Pepper looked particularly scared and grabbed me and wouldn't let go.

"We're gettin' out of here, Pepper," James whispered. How he said it let me know he was serious. No more talking about getting out . . . we're doing it . . . and soon. He looked at me and stuck out his fist. I bopped it with mine and looked back down at the box.

"It's been ten minutes, I bet," Pepper said.

I pulled out the instructions. What I read though had nothing to do with applying burn cream.

Chapter 14

WE GOTTA GET OUTTA THIS PLACE

I read the instructions and re-focused my eyes. I looked at James and handed him the little paper. He read it and his eyes also looked confused. Then he whispered it out loud. "Green '56 Chevy in parking lot. Key under mat."

Pepper lifted her head. "What?" James showed her the slip of paper. "Where'd that come from?" she asked. I held up the ointment box.

"Might be a trap," James said, but he didn't sound convinced of that.

Someone suddenly was messing with the door and I stashed the paper under the bed foam. It swung open and Mikey stood filling the narrow gap, holding sandwiches and a jug of water. He didn't say anything; he just handed us the food and water and left.

We each slept in little shifts and, on mine, I put my ear to the door. I didn't hear anything. I was trying to picture where all those Carters were sleeping. I knew there was another berth in the aft of the boat.

They must all be stuffed in there, like sardines, I thought.

I looked out the porthole and all I saw was the light on the shore. No movement. I gently shook James and held my finger to my lips. I pointed to the hatch and unlocked it. James pushed on it but it didn't open.

I got right up to his ear. "Sometimes they're just sticky," I whispered. "Let me try." I wedged my belt buckle under the lip and pried. It gave a low thunk when it gave way and we both dropped down and faked sleeping. No one came in and no one opened the hatch. He tapped me, we tried again, and the hatch gave way with a sticky peeling sound.

I winced and looked at James. It was free, but I let it down.

"Let me have a look," James whispered very low. I nodded and we opened the lid.

"Careful. Don't let it fall back," I said, in my smallest whisper. James stood on the bunks and raised himself up and swirled his head back and forth. Then slowly dropped back down.

"Looks clear," he said. "I think we should *all* go."

"All of us? Are you sure?" I asked. Every time we'd talked about it, we had agreed that there was a better chance of just one of us escaping. But also, what happens to the two who are left? That was always the big question when we'd been batting the options back and forth.

"It looks all clear. I think we can do it," he whispered. "It's now or never, Cal."

I looked up at the thick mess of stars framed by the square hole in the roof. Yup. It was now or never, alright. I wanted off that boat—away from Carmelita and all her crazy Carter clan—so bad that I was willing to swim in the Columbia River . . . at night. James woke Pepper and shushed her before she could speak.

"Time to go, Pepps," he whispered to her.

"You're first, Cal," James said.

"You said you were first," I argued.

"Changed my mind. If there's trouble, I want you two outta here," he said. I wanted to object, but he shook his head no and pointed at the hole in the roof. I stood on the bunks and slowly inched up and peered around the deck. Everything seemed quiet, so I signaled and James helped shove me up and onto the deck. Pepper's head then appeared and she looked around too, but I grabbed her and helped pull her up. Her foot "clunked" the hull and I gave her the stink eye. Sorry, she said with her eyes. James then started to climb up but I heard a voice.

"Where you think yer goin'?" the voice snarled. James struggled but he was being held from below.

"Run," James yelled at me and Pepper in a hushed voice. I didn't though. Instead I tried to pull him free. I couldn't do it; whoever had him clamped in their arms wasn't letting go. I jumped up and grabbed Pepper and shoved her over the side and hurled myself into the black water after her. That's when I learned Pepper could hardly swim. She instantly started thrashing and grabbing me. She pulled me under and I barely got away from her. When we popped back to the surface, people were running around on the boat. Somehow James had gotten free and flung himself over the side. But then I heard another splash. Derrick had jumped in after him.

I looked back and they were wrestling in the water. Someone else went in and they soon had James back to the boat.

I had to dunk Pepper to calm her down. I'd learned this life saving technique in swimming class, but never in a million years did I think I'd ever be using it. Especially with people chasing me.

"Wadda you doing?" Pepper screamed at me, and tried to hit me.

"Grab my shirt and hold on," I ordered.

Luckily she wasn't completely panicked and latched onto my shoulders with a death-grip. I started kicking toward the shore.

"Trust me, and lay back." She did, but she was breathing hard from fear. Well, we both were. I got us moving forward with the breast stroke and her feet trailed back.

"Kick, Pepper, kick," I said, gasping for air. She did, but was now kicking me in the stomach. I didn't care, though, she was adding power.

I grabbed a quick glance behind us and Carmelita was on the deck barking orders. You'd think a war had just broke out and a thousand troops were storming over the hill.

"You morons," she screamed. "Who let . . . get that

anchor . . . where's the key to the engine? No one checked the hatch? You boys are idiots!"

The Carter boys on board were dragging James back on the boat when Carmelita shouted, "Get in the water, Cletus!"

I heard him shout something, then a big splash. I glanced back and Cletus was dog paddling.

"I'll get 'em," Derrick shouted. He jumped off the boat and started swimming after us.

Someone got the engine started, but the anchor wasn't up and the boat twisted around on the anchor line. There was a lot more yelling and screaming about that. I was pretty sure Carmelita was going to blow a gasket.

I was pulling water harder than I'd ever pulled before. The fact that I was swimming in black water, at night, didn't even phase me. I was worried that my arms were going to fall off, and I could feel my legs wanting to cramp.

"I dunno if I can make it," I said, completely out of breath.

"You've got to, Cal. He's getting closer!"

I glanced back. Derrick was gaining on us, while Cletus was way back thrashing and plowing through the water. I had to dig deeper.

Although I had no time to think, I was worried about James. Now that Carmelita was all stirred up again, she might just tell her crazy boys to tear him apart and dump him in the river. This is exactly what we'd talked about if we didn't all go.

I grunted and pulled harder against the cold water. Suddenly, Pepper's butt and my knees hit sand. Our strength was nearly gone, but we sloshed out onto the shore and started running.

"Head toward that light in the parking lot," I yelled. Then I heard a low scraping sound and looked back. The boat had hit bottom and was stuck.

"Reverse," I heard Carmelita scream. "REVERSE!" I saw

her shoving someone out of the way and start working the controls, yelling orders and pumping a fist in the air in anger. The engines reversed and gunned.

We reached the gravel parking area and saw three cars in the lot—Derrick's Ford truck, a Buick, and the '56 Chevy. I found the key under the matt and the Chevy started right up. I jammed it into gear and revved the engine. That's when we saw Derrick hit the parking area. I popped the clutch and the tires spit gravel, the old Chevy fishtailing just as Derrick reached for us. All he could do was slap the car as we sped past him. I nearly ran him over, which I thought would have been great. Instead, he charged off toward his truck.

Pepper yelled at me, "He's after us!"

I had the pedal to the floor, but had no idea which way to go. I was skidding around the sharp curves that I hoped would get us out of the little picnic park. We doubled back around and could see Derrick tear out of the parking area. The road suddenly ended at a tee. I chose left, thinking that would at least take us back toward The Dalles. It was Highway 99; a little two-lane road that ran alongside the river. The Chevy had a huge steering wheel and I was sitting down lower than in Gramps' Dodge, so I had to get up very straight to see over the wheel and the dash. Pepper was facing backwards, giving me the play-by-play.

"Here he comes," she said. I glanced in the mirror and she was right; he made the turn onto the highway and was fishtailing as he stomped on the gas.

She suddenly stiffened and leaned over the seat. "Hey, there's another car following him!"

I risked a glance in the mirror. Who's that? I asked myself.

Derrick's V8 Ford was eating up the distance between us because the Chevy was an old six cylinder.

"He's gonna run us down," I said, looking back.

"How far to The Dalles?" Pepper asked. She was sitting

backwards, leaning over the seat, watching Derrick and now the other car.

"Dunno . . . a ways," I guessed.

"He's getting closer," Pepper shouted.

I stopped slowing down on the curves and Pepper—trying to keep watch—slammed into me, then the door. It took everything I had to keep the Chevy on the road. I nearly lost control on every turn and kept crossing the yellow line. It was the middle of the night, so we only passed a couple of cars. They had to swerve into the gravel to get out of my way and I swerved too. One time the Chevy went up on two wheels.

"That other car is trying to pass Derrick," Pepper screamed and scrambled into the backseat. "It's trying to get in front of Derrick. It slammed him. I think it's that Buick. Maybe it's Doctor Floyd!"

I didn't answer, having decided that I needed to concentrate on what was in front of us and not what was happening back there. I had a little experience in fast cars and didn't want to crash again. But, after tearing around curves and barely missing going off the road, I started to get the feel for the Chevy. I figured out just how much I needed to let off the gas on certain curves and when to stomp on it again. The road was never straight, so I couldn't hardly ever see what was going on behind me. But Pepper kept yelling out what was happening with the Ford and the Buick.

"Wow!" she shouted. Then, "OHHH NOOOO! They crashed. Now they're off the road. Step on it, Calvin!"

I glanced in the mirror and didn't see any lights. I kept the pedal down, but felt a tiny bit of hope and relief. Pepper turned around and flopped down in the seat. "We made it," she cheered and grabbed me around the neck.

"Hey," I yelled, "Maybe."

My eyes kept jumping to the mirrors. Pepper bounced up and looked back again, too.

"Ah oh," she said. "Someone's coming." I'd halfway expected it.

Headlights swerved around a corner and fishtailed back and forth. I figured it was Derrick again. Who else would it be?

I quit slowing down on the curves and kept my speed up. It didn't matter, though, that Ford had too much power and caught up. It slammed into our trunk, causing the Chevy to swerve and skid. I tried my best to keep control of it, but Derrick kept slamming into the Chevy again and again making it jig and jag. Around one curve, he hit me just right and the car started to slide sideways. I spun the wheel and we skidded the other way and then I felt the car roll up on its wheels.

Everything went into slow motion. Pepper flew into the front seat and hit the dashboard. My feet sailed out to the side and hit her. My hands held onto the wheel, but had no effect. I saw the road coming toward me through the driver-side window. The road in front of me tilted and tilted and then was sideways.

My window shattered and gravel was pelting me in the face. The horrible scraping sound of that old Chevy skidding and rolling across the gravel was all I could hear. If we were screaming, I couldn't tell. Then, the passenger door flew open and Pepper disappeared. I watched my hand let go of the steering wheel and grab at air. Cattails and weeds whipped through my window, slapping me in the face and then the front of the car splashed into some kind of pond and thudded to a stop. It got suddenly quiet, except for a hissing sound. The Chevy was on its side and I was wadded up in a knot on the floor. Gravel crunched when Derrick's Ford skidded to a stop. A door slammed and then I heard the crunch of Derrick's feet on gravel. His face appeared, looking at me through the shattered windshield. The broken glass made him look splintered into a hundred pieces. I think he smiled, and motioned if I needed help, but didn't do anything. He just casually lit up a cigarette.

A car's lights, way down the road, swept across the scene and he looked back. He looked back at me and then disappeared. His tires spit gravel and then it was quiet again, except for that hissing sound. I slowly untangled myself and stood up and poked my head through the passenger door. When I got myself on top of the car, I fell off and landed with a painful thud. Gas smell was everywhere so I started to crawl and was limping away from the car when it suddenly exploded into a ball of flames.

I spun around and held up my arm against the heat. The whole back of the car was burning. I stumbled further away from the heat and that's when I saw Pepper. She was lying in the cattails, near the water. I hurried over to her and pulled her away from the fire and checked if she was breathing. She was, but she was scraped up pretty bad. Her eyes fluttered opened and she wanted to get up.

"No, no, hold still for a minute. Let me see how bad you're hurt." I held her hand for a second until she laid back down.

"Ooooh," she moaned.

I looked closely. "Anything broken, you think?" She moved a little and shook her head, no. But she had plenty of cuts on her arms and face. I scooted close and laid her head in my lap. The flames were warm and lit our faces, and we waited. Pepper started to cry a little and I wrapped my arm around her. When the car arrived, it skidded to a stop and a man and a woman sprinted toward us.

"Oh Gosh," the woman screamed. "Do something, Casey," she yelled at the man. Casey dropped to his knees.

"What happened?" he asked. But he didn't really wait for an answer. He said to the woman, "There's a blanket in the trunk . . . and a first aid kit." She ran back to their car. "Bring the water, too!" he shouted after her. "Okay, kids. We're here . . ." but then looked around. "Where's your parents?" he asked and jumped up. "Are they in the car?"

he yelled.

"No, just us. It's just us, Mister." I moaned, then petered out and slumped forward, still holding Pepper.

Another car screeched to a stop and a man jumped out. He tried spraying a fire extinguisher, but the fire was too big and it quickly ran out. There was a bunch of shouting and talking as this new man and the first couple decided what should be done. Between the three of them, they got us loaded into the man's station wagon and on our way to The Dalles. We were both wet and cold from our swim. Pepper was shaking and her teeth were chattering, so the woman wrapped her in a blanket and held her close.

Getting to The Dalles at sixty miles per hour didn't take long. On the way I tried my best to explain what had happened and that James was still on the Carter's boat, and how that was not a good thing. Also, that Derrick Carter's the person who ran us off the road. The woman kept saying, "Oh my gosh," and "it's a wonder you're both still alive." The driver listened and nodded his head, and said he would call the police as soon as we got to the hospital. When the man skidded the station wagon into the emergency entrance, things started to happen fast. Me and Pepper were rushed in and smothered in attention. The woman with Casey, who we found out was named Jean, stuck to Pepper like glue, and Casey tried to get a hold of Gram and Uncle Neal, but there wasn't any answer. I was suddenly worried about Gram and that they were still in White Salmon. The other man had called the police and when they arrived, they started asking a mess of questions. After they left, it was late, so I didn't hear anything more about what happened until the next day.

Pepper needed fifty stitches and a mess of bandages for all her wounds. I was twisted and bent in places that weren't meant to bend, but I wasn't broken anywhere. Just a lot of scrapes and cuts and my burns from the night before. My eyes went blurry and crossed a few times, which was interesting. Sometimes there were more nurses in the room than I thought could fit. Then my eyes would straighten out.

The next day, they decided to move us to Hood River. Casey, the man who first stopped, phoned Gram and Uncle Neal. When I asked him what Uncle Neal had said, he made a funny face and wouldn't tell me. I knew I was on deck for hours of lectures and stinky faces.

When Gram and Uncle Neal finally got to the hospital and I saw how worried Gram was, and that she'd been crying, that took the cake. Uncle Neal could lecture me, spank me, ship me off to Canada . . . just so Gram would stop being sad. Every time she went to the bathroom or stepped outside to talk to a doctor or the nurse, Uncle Neal got a head-start on skinning me. It was going to take him a while, I knew, because he was going to do it a few inches at a time.

Chapter 15

GOOD DREAMS GONE BAD

Most of the time my head felt gummy from the pain pills my nurses kept slipping me. I had a hard time staying awake and sometimes I wasn't quite sure if the strange dream-like visions I was having were real.

That's what was happening when James slipped into my room and closed the door. I wasn't sure it was really him or just me wanting to see him.

"Wanna go outside and throw the football?" he asked with a big grin on his face.

"Whhhaaattt?" I asked. I could hear that even my words were gummy, which made James laugh.

"Or, maybe we ride up to the mine and you-know-what," he whispered.

I looked at him and tried to focus my eyes. He looked a bit wavy and I couldn't sort out what he meant.

"Whhaatt's I-know-what?" I slurred. He chuckled again.

"Okay, I'll leave you alone," he said and pulled over a chair.

He seemed to be moving so slow . . .

"Guess what," he continued in a low, excited voice. "Carmelita and her bunch a monkey boys are all in jail."

"They are?" I slurred.

"Everyone except Derrick and Cletus. Somehow that Cletus got to shore and didn't get picked up. Derrick disappeared after running you guys off the road."

"I mean, you and yer girlfriend?" he giggled. I don't know what kind of face I made, but he laughed at that too.

"Funny," I snickered, my mind starting to clear. "Where is Pepper?"

"On the second floor. She's doin' okay after they sewed her back together." He started fiddling around with a gizmo the nurses used to check my breathing. "They're gonna keep you guys for a few more days, I think."

"How'd you get off the boat?" I mumbled.

"Idiots ran aground when the cops were chasing us. Wham, right on the rocks. Dead stop and we all flew forward."

He was smiling as his arms shot up in the air.

"Then everyone bailed overboard and left me tied up down in that little room with water pouring in and the door locked."

James was now sounding more mad than scared about the ordeal.

My eyes flew open wide.

"Yeah," he continued, "up to my chin when someone finally came down and got me." James ran his hand along his chin to show me how high the water got. He then pulled out a newspaper article and pointed to the few pictures.

"There's the boat, half sunk on the rocks. There's Carmelita being put in the police car. That's me, wrapped in a blanket." I could tell he was proud to again have his picture in the paper. He tossed it on the bed and leaned in close.

"When you get outta here, we gotta get back up to the Magpie," James whispered. "After all this commotion, I'm worried Derrick's gonna get up there and figure it all out. He probably has Cletus tied up somewhere right now and torturing him for the story."

My head was clearing a little and I realized now why James wanted to get back to the mine.

"I think we should just forget about that chest," I said, my voice still slow and drooling.

His head was shaking, no.

"Cut the cake how you want, Cal; I'll never forget about it."

James looked at the clock.

"I better get going. I hitched a ride down with Burley and his mom and I gotta meet 'em at four." He slugged me in the shoulder, which hurt, and he realized it. "Oh, sorry." He then fake-punched me in the chin and hurried out the door.

Later, when my nurse came in, she commented about us being very lucky to have gotten away from those Carters. My night-time nurse said it'd been a nasty bit of business out there on the river. The sheriff chased them in their boat for a few miles, until the Carters ran up on some rocks that were just under the surface. Then it'd been a mess of Carters jumping overboard and leaving James tied up down below. I didn't tell her I knew all that. I was hoping she'd spill other news that I didn't know.

Even though he'd had a scare, stuck in a sinking boat, James loved it. He loved a good story to tell at school or at camp fires, and it really helped when we were in the paper, which had happened before. That way it was real and we didn't have to bring it up; kids just surrounded us and asked a million questions.

Right now, though, I was glad to be away from those Carters and in a warm bed. I didn't want anything more to do with them. Even just talking about them and what they'd done would make me sleep with a flashlight for a while.

* * *

When nothing much happens, you notice any little thing that does. What I mean is; being in the hospital is just plain boring unless someone's visiting. When no one's around, whatever's going on out in the hall is about the only excitement. My nurses never closed my door because they were always peeking in to see how I was doing. That was just fine with me; my door was my window to all the hospital hubbub.

This wasn't my first time in the hospital either. When I was about five, my tonsils about blew up and they took them out. And then when I was around seven and red-hot with pneumonia, they parked me in the hospital for a few days. And another time when me and James got tangled up with some thieves and ended up in a bad car wreck, we both spent a few days patched up in the White Salmon hospital. Yep, I knew about lying around for hours and hours, waiting to go home. It's also why I knew how hospitals work.

During the day all kinds of people are around. Relatives visiting patients. Pastors. The police. And all the nurses and doctors. Things are different at night. The only people walking up and down the halls and coming into the rooms are dressed in white. So, a guy in jeans and a jacket pushing a wheelchair is unusual . . . he got my attention. I knew I wasn't dreaming because, sick of feeling foggy, I'd skipped those sleeping pills.

I wasn't really looking at the door when he first passed by; that's why I'd only caught a glimpse. Now I stared at the hall. Then the cigarette smell drifted into my room. Normally that wasn't anything. Lots of people smoked. But not in a hospital. The hair on my neck stood up when the man suddenly reappeared and pushed the wheelchair into my room, quietly shutting the door. The light was dim and I closed down my eyes to slits to look asleep.

It was Derrick! I felt a shot of fear and my heart jumped into high gear. James said the police hadn't found him.

He stepped up close, fumbled with my chart, and then shook my leg.

"Hello, Calvin Poag," he whispered, kind of laughing.

"Time to wake up."

Still pretending to sleep, I slowly snuck my hand toward the nurse's button, but he grabbed my wrist and clamped it tight. I winced.

"Eh, eh, eh. Three's a crowd," he chuckled. Derrick Carter really loved his own jokes. He laughed at them every time.

"Wanna go for a ride?" he asked and jiggled the wheelchair. "I hear kids love these things."

He gave my wrist a tug. "I checked yer chart there, and I'm thinkin' it's discharge time."

Derrick asking me if I wanted to go for a ride sounded more like, "Wanna stick your arm in a saw blade?"

I tried to yank my arm free, but it hurt because of my strained wrist.

"Come on," he whispered. "I asked yer Grandma if you could come out and play." He was trying to sound fun and playful. It wasn't working because he really just sounded dangerous. His eyebrows lifted up, all surprised that I didn't want to go with him.

"No? Well, what if I told you we were going do a little shooting?" He lifted his shirt and I saw the butt of a gun. He suddenly got very serious.

"Normally, I don't shoot much indoors; it's so dang noisy. Though, I could make an exception."

I shifted my legs and sat up. It hurt to move.

"Oh, does that hurt? Did you get a boo-boo when our cars bumped?"

He followed a chuckle with a sneer.

"Okay Calvin, let's not make this any more interesting than it has to be. Hop onboard and we'll go for a little spin."

I decided I didn't want to find out what Derrick's idea of "interesting" meant, so I got in the chair and he got down close to my ear.

"Now, we're gonna take a stroll right on outta here." His breath was stale from cigarettes and Juicy Fruit gum. It made my nose turn up.

"I'll have my little squirt gun handy if you decide you wanna create a scene." He poked me in the back with his finger and gave a little laugh.

He opened the door, peeked out, and rolled me quickly away from the nurse's station.

As I told you, nothing much goes on in hospitals at night, so no one saw us until we got to the elevators. An old man was mopping the floor and he glanced up. I could see that he thought it was strange, us being out past visiting hours. He looked at me and then up at Derrick behind him. His mouth kind of shifted to the side and he glanced back down at me. I tried to make a face that said S-O-S, but he didn't get it and just went back to work. On the ground floor, Derrick turned away from the front desk and down a deserted hall and sped me through a side door. The cool air hit me in the face and jolted me more awake.

"You're not going to get away with this, you know," I said.

"Says you, the little man with no plan," he said and snorted out a laugh while shoving me across a parking lot. Then I saw Cletus climb out of the Carter's Plymouth. He opened the back door and they manhandled me into the backseat. Instantly, I noticed the smells—mold and cat pee mixed with used oil. The seats were worn and torn and a few springs were trying to escape. Which is exactly what I wanted to do.

"Watch him," Derrick ordered Cletus, and hurried back to the building with the wheelchair. Cletus grabbed the scruff of my hospital gown and casually waited. It was dead quiet, except for Cletus' thick breathing, and the parking lot was empty. If someone had come along I would have made some kind of commotion; there just isn't anything happening in White Salmon after around eleven o'clock at night.

"How'd you get away from the police?" I tried to sound

casual. You know, just making conversation.

"Jus' did," he answered, and didn't offer any more details. He didn't even look at me. Just stared out the window and waited for Derrick. I also started to wonder where he was.

"How long's it take to dump off a wheelchair?" I muttered.

Just then, the hospital door opened and I saw Derrick wheeling Pepper across the parking lot.

Instinctively, I reached for the door handle, but Cletus grabbed me and hauled me back into the seat. Derrick had Pepper by the hair with a hand over her mouth to keep her quiet. Because she was squirming to break free, he threatened and struggled trying to get her into the front seat. For a twelve-year-old, Pepper was strong . . . and tough.

When Cletus opened his door to try and help Derrick, I realized that their scuffling gave me an opportunity to escape. I thought about running, but what would happen to Pepper? Also, I was sure that I couldn't outrun Derrick in a hospital gown . . . and he had that gun.

"I hate you, Derrick Carter," Pepper shouted when they finally managed to get her into the front seat. Cletus kept her door shut while Derrick ran around to the driver's side. As soon as he got in, Pepper tried to reach across the seat and hit him. Derrick just laughed, jammed the car in gear, and hurried out of the parking lot. She shouted a few other things and tried again to hit Derrick, but Cletus reached up front and pulled her back, using his giant arms to keep her in place.

Then Derrick asked, "Hey Pepper, where's your big brother? At home? Roaming around town? Maybe he's camping? I just don't know." Derrick looked over the seat at me. "Anything you can add to that, Calvin?"

"Maybe he's with the police," I said, trying to sound belligerent. "Maybe they're watching every move you make."

"Don't think so, but nice try," Derrick said.

"Yeah, nice try, Dumbo," Cletus agreed. "Cuz he's at our hunting camp."

As Cletus added his goofy huffy-bear laugh, Derrick stomped on the brakes . . . all of us flying forward. He turned and glared at Cletus.

"Can you just go ten minutes without saying something stupid or spoiling all the fun?"

"Well, he is," Cletus whined.

"Well he is," Derrick also whined, mocking Cletus. Cletus punched the seat and Derrick whipped around again.

"You got somethin' on yer thick-headed mind, Cuz?" he growled. Cletus quickly slumped back into his seat.

"No," he mumbled.

"Then keep yer mouth shut," Derrick ordered, hitting the gas pedal so hard that the Plymouth peeled out.

"Where's the hunting camp?" Pepper asked Derrick.

He didn't answer . . .

Chapter 16

HOOLIGANS' HIDEAWAY

The Carter's hunting camp was nothing more than a scrappy little cabin tucked back off an old logging road. It would have been great for me and James as a hideout or a fort, but it was really just a place to throw down sleeping bags and get warm after tramping around in the woods all day. There wasn't much inside—a little stove, low bunks, and a wobbly table.

Derrick swung open the door and followed me inside. His flashlight found James lying on his side in a corner; a handkerchief gagging his mouth. Whoever had tied him up had basically rolled him in ropes. It was obvious that he'd been trying to get free because he was covered in dirt and dust.

James' eyes popped open when he heard Pepper being dragged in by Cletus.

"Umbleegumaa," he said through the gag.

"I know, he does look cute in a dress," Derrick laughed while pointing at me. He shoved us down on a bunk and tied our feet. Meanwhile, Cletus stoked the fire and lit a lamp while chortling at his cousin's joke about my hospital gown.

"Well, someone's been having a lot a fun, I see," Derrick said and righted a chair James had knocked over. "Get him back in his corner," he ordered. Cletus roughly grabbed James and propped him by the stove.

James looked fine. He hadn't been hurt, anyway.

Derrick took a few steps and stopped, directly in front of me.

"I know how good those doctors were treating you,

Calvin, and how much yer ready to go for a sprint. But, I sure don't want you to hurt yourself. My unprofessional recommendation is don't try and run away."

All smiles, he patted me on top of the head, then sat right next to Pepper and put his arm around her shoulder. "Cuz I got me some insurance."

She tried to squirm away, but he held her tight, then looked at me and James.

"Now, let's talk about my chest of coins," he said, showing us his horrible yellow, pointy teeth. He walked over and yanked off James' gag, which instantly started a bunch of shouting and arguing about how things were gonna be. Then he was back onto the mine and his treasure chest.

"I been tellin' you, we don't know nothin' about a chest," James growled. He was playing dumb and I followed his lead. But Derrick was getting more and more irritated and irrational. One minute he'd be mister funny man and then he'd throw a little fit and toss something across the cabin. The whole time Cletus was nervous and chewing his nails. His head swiveled back and forth as if he was at a tennis match.

Derrick turned toward Pepper.

"What about you, Little Miss? Who rides all the way up into the mountains, on a Sunday night, by herself, if she don't have some idea of what's at the other end of that long, scary ride?"

He looked at his cousin.

"Don't you agree, Cleets?"

Cletus nodded. "Long bike ride," he agreed.

"Not for me," Pepper said, proud of herself. It was true. She'd tagged right along on those goofy rides we took her on and she kept up the whole time.

"James and Cal do fun stuff and I wanted to come with."

"Yeah," said Derrick, "and you had no idea what kind a fun stuff yer boys here were up to?" Pepper shook her head, no.

Derrick lit up a cigarette. The tiny cabin quickly filled with smoke and made my eyes water.

"We don't know nothin' about coins," James said. "Whatever happened, it wasn't us."

"That's not what the big man here says," Derrick barked.

Cletus winced.

"Two guys, Dee . . . but it was dark . . . two guys is what I saw," Cletus said, his voice trailing off to a scruffy whisper.

"Twwwooo guys," Derrick repeated. "These two guys?"

"Maybe."

Derrick squeezed Pepper's shoulder.

"You don't think it's a strange coincidence that this little runt is that one's sister? And this other runt is that one's pal?"

Derrick loosened his grip on Pepper and gave me a shove.

"Pretty neat little set, if you ask me," Derrick added while surveying us, his prisoners.

"Cletus," he growled, "you told me these two clowns were up at the mine. And you seen 'em. These two guys!" He got in Cletus' face. Cletus cowered and looked at the floor while nodding, yes.

Derrick stepped over and grabbed James by the collar and lifted him off the floor and sat him in the chair.

"Then, you blew up our house," he yelled. "But there's just something I can't figure, Cleets." He turned to look at Cletus, his voice now low and dangerous. "Why were you up at the mine?"

Cletus got restless and his hands shot down between his knees and his head wagged from side to side. He was trying not to look at Derrick, but Derrick dropped James and stepped into his view.

"Up at the mine when you stumbled onto the little redhead girl, Cleets. Why?" His eyebrows shot up as if he had just figured something out. "Was someone stickin' his hand in the cookie jar?"

I couldn't help it, a snort-laugh burst out of my mouth. Then James also spit one out. I was suddenly worried we both were going to launch into an unstoppable sleep-over laughing fit. Derrick turned his head and looked at us.

"I know, it's hilarious. I can't hardly keep from laughing too," Derrick grumbled and smiled. He looked crazy . . . his eyes were wide open and his nasty teeth seemed ready to bite someone.

He turned back to Cletus.

"I'm just so snoopy about what was going on up at the ol' mine while I was off doin' business. Feelin' snoopy, I is. You know hows I gets when I'm feelin' snoopy."

Cletus looked nervous and sweaty as Derrick bobbed around the tiny cabin, trying to get him to spill the beans about his solo trek to the mine. Every now and then Derrick's shirt would lift up and remind everyone that he had a gun. The moment James saw the silver snub-nose, his eyes had magnetically locked onto it.

Derrick suddenly let out an exasperated sigh. "I gotta go see a man about a horse," he said and stomped out the door.

"He's sure hard on you, Cletus," James whispered. "Yeah," muttered Pepper. Cletus glanced at her.

"What a jerk, Cletus?" James added. Cletus looked at the door and mashed up his face. I thought he was going to cry. He nodded his head.

"I thought so," James said real soft. Pepper was watching Cletus and touched his arm with her hand.

"I'll bet he's rough on everyone," James said while leaning closer to Cletus. "Sometimes you just gotta, you know, do something right."

I could tell that James was about to offer an idea when Derrick burst through the door, zipping up his pants. He seemed all excited and happy. He was grinning and zeroed in on Cletus.

"Yer smarter than I thought, Cousin. Yup, a real genius." Derrick pulled out his gun, pointing it at the floor.

"Hey, I have a great idea," he said, all excited. "Okay everyone, we're goin' on a field trip! Gonna go see what we can see. And find out what we can find out."

Derrick grabbed me and Pepper and yanked us to our feet.

"Get Mr. Big mouth there," he snapped at Cletus, looking at James. Then it was a bunch of shoving and rough treatment as they muscled us out the door.

Chapter 17

AND THEN A FIGHT BROKE OUT

In the car, Pepper was between me and Cletus in the back seat. James was in the front, still tied up. Derrick was driving.

"Hey, how about untying my feet?" James asked. He swung his legs around so Derrick could untie them. Derrick just laughed and shoved them away.

"Yup. I figure stuff out, kids," Derrick said. He was sounding thoughtful again. We were bumping down some old logging road and he had his right arm on the seat, all casual. "Momma likes that about me. I help make her plans, you see." He glanced over at James and then back at us, then in the mirror at Cletus. "Right, Cleets?" Cletus didn't respond. He'd lost interest in the conversation and was staring out the window into the blackness.

"Ah Cleets, come on . . . don't be a baby. You know how I hate it when you cry."

Derrick smirked and slapped the steering wheel.

"Everyone," he continued, "if Cletus starts crying, just let him go until he's done leaking. It might take a while 'cause he's a real big boy with a real big water tank." Another big joke. I glanced at Cletus, and sure enough, his eyes were getting wet. Pepper was looking at him too.

"That's a mean thing to say," she said, still looking at Cletus. She then put her hand on his arm. Cletus glanced down and then at Pepper. His face was all wet from tears. I elbowed her. She elbowed me back. James looked over the seat and his eyes popped open when he saw what was going on. Derrick glanced in the mirror and groaned.

"Good grief, Pepper," Derrick grumbled. "You two gonna

get married or what?"

"Shud-up, Dee," Cletus mumbled.

"Yeah, shut up," Pepper chimed in. I kept my eyes on the mirror and Derrick's face. He was grinning.

"You always wanted a little sister, Cleets. Maybe youse finally got one," he crowed and laughed.

"She's always been good with people no one appreciates," James said. Cletus looked at James and then at Pepper. Tears really started to flow now. In fact, his chest started to shake and Pepper scooted closer and leaned against his huge shoulder. I couldn't believe what I was seeing. And then it hit me—James, with Pepper's help, was working up some of his magic sauce, some kind of strategy on ol' Cletus that might give us an opportunity in the near future. After all, coming up with an instant story was kind of James' specialty. I just had to be on my toes to go along with whatever he was planning.

"What kind of deal do you have with Cletus?" James asked Derrick.

Even in the dark, I could see Derrick's face tighten up and his hands grip the steering wheel.

"That's it, isn't it?" James continued. "He's the muscle and you're the brains. One for him and three for you."

Derrick's arm shot out and backhanded James.

"Whatever deal I got with Cletus is our deal," he snarled. "Right, Cleets?"

Derrick looked in the mirror.

"But we got a problem, don't we, Cleets . . ."

I could tell Derrick had reached the end of his joking around.

"It ain't easy to figure what to do when you find yer cousin's hand in the cookie jar," he snarled before turning his attention to James. "What am I gonna do with him, anyway?"

"Give him his fair share," James mumbled. I looked at Cletus and he was now very interested in this conversation.

He'd stopped crying, but was still holding Pepper's hand. I quickly looked away and tried to keep a straight face. I couldn't believe it. Cletus was untying Pepper's hands.

Derrick reached over and back-handed James. "Wadda you know about fair shares?"

Even though James was tied up, he's no one to mess with. Derrick had his hands full trying to drive and pound his passenger, the car swerving off what little road there was while hitting pot holes and berms.

Suddenly, I saw that the road was about to end.

"Look out!"

Derrick glanced forward and slammed on the brakes. We all crashed into the seat and James hit the dashboard. Pepper's hands were free and she started working on my knots. In a split second I recognized that we were at the road to the mine. But that's the only split second I got to think about it because Derrick yanked out his gun and pointed it at James, who ducked. He then swung it around at us. Pepper screamed and Cletus lunged across the seat and grabbed for the gun. BOOM! It sounded like a cannon inside the car. I felt the wind of the bullet whiz past my ear. Cletus had Derrick around the neck and was trying to pull him back across the seat. As they fought, the car rocked.

BOOM! Derrick's gun went off again and Cletus lurched, but didn't let go. His anger turned into a rage.

"I'm gonna kill you," Cletus screamed.

My hands were still tied, but I grabbed the door handle and exploded out of the car, followed by Pepper. "Run," I ordered in a harsh whisper as she took off for the trees. I jerked open James' door and tried dragging him out. Derrick yelled and his gun waved in our direction, but Cletus was keeping him busy. Derrick had to let go of James and I pulled him out. He landed on the ground with a thud and I started dragging him away from the car. Pepper ran back and helped me. We could still hear Derrick and Cletus struggling and thrashing around inside the car as we got untied.

The three of us ran into the dark forest and, suddenly, my right foot slipped—probably on the root of a tree—and I fell sideways to the ground. I was okay, but my foot was throbbing . . . and swelling. James helped me up and I was able to stand, but moving was hindered by a painful limp.

Immediately, James hoisted me on his shoulder and carried me deeper into the trees. Then we heard another distant crack of a gunshot.

"I sure hope that was Cletus doing the shooting," James said. He found us a place behind a big rotten log and we hunkered down to rest. Both me and Pepper were exhausted. James wrapped his thin coat around Pepper and I had to tough it out.

"Now what?" I asked. We were all scared and James kept looking back over the log.

"We gotta run, guys," Pepper whispered.

"Yeah, but where?" I asked, trying to massage a tender ankle.

"Ta get the coins," James said.

"Now? I'm a little hobbled here, James."

"Do you see where we are, Cal? A half mile from the mine, at the most."

"James, Derrick just shot Cletus . . . I think . . . and probably wants to shoot us all. Let's get outta here! We can come back when things calm down."

"Things aren't going to calm down, Cal. I guess you haven't been paying close attention." He glared at me and waved his hand back in the direction of the car. "That crazy guy's not calming down."

I didn't know what to say. He was right. Derrick was a maniac and all he cared about was getting that chest back.

"I have to do this, Cal. I told you, my family's got no money."

He looked at Pepper. "Derrick and Cletus buried a chest with a bunch of old coins and we found it and hid it."

"James wants it to help your mom," I added.

"I can't carry it by myself, Cal. If I don't do something, we're gonna be living on the streets in Hood River or worse."

All I could think about was Derrick coming after us . . . with his gun.

"If yer not coming, then I'm going by myself," James said. "I'll figure it out. I always do."

"Well, I'm coming with," Pepper said.

"It's now or never, Cal," James added.

"I know," I muttered while getting up. "It always is with us."

"I'm coming with," Pepper said again. It was not a question. She was coming with us.

"Yeah. You're comin' with, Pepps," James said and gave her a little hug.

Chapter 18

THIS FREE RIDE IS PAINFUL

Bouncing on James' shoulders through the woods was killing all my sore spots. I could see that Pepper was trying with all she had to keep up. None of us talked until we struck the road that led to the mine. Then he let me down like a sack of potatoes.

"We're getting close," he whispered. He was looking up and down the road. I was looking at the ground, and I could hardly breathe. "Can you make it?" he asked. All I did was nod my head. He hoisted me back on his shoulders.

I've always known James was stronger than most of us in the ninth grade. But carrying me through the woods, in the middle of the night, was something I never imagined could happen. But he had a purpose, and James with a purpose is hard to contain. I've said that a bunch of times, I think, but it's why he leads and I generally follow. Right now, though, I didn't have any choice. Keeping to the woods, James skirted the road the whole half mile.

"We don't have a light," I said, when the practical part of my brain started to think about what was next.

"I know. I've been thinking about that," James said. "If we can build a little fire, we can carry it with us in one those old shovels we found." I nodded, okay. It was just getting a fire going, I thought, with Derrick shooting at us and Cletus lumbering around like a bear, trying to decide which side he was now on.

"What if Derrick's already there?" I asked.

"I dunno yet. But between the two of us . . . ."

"Three of us," Pepper interrupted.

"Right. Three of us, we'll figure something."

Thirty yards and a hundred bounces later, I nudged James on his shoulder. "Listen," I said through puffs of wind. "Do you hear that?"

"Sounds like a car," said Pepper.

Chapter 19

BLOOD IN THE HEADLIGHTS

While we were hunkered down, the Plymouth sped by. I could see only Derrick in the glow of the dash lights. When I mentioned that, James said, "Cletus might be shot and on the floor." That got Pepper upset and she started to cry.

"Pepps," James said. "No crying or being a baby. This is not gonna be easy and we need you to be with us. You hear?"

She nodded her head and sucked in the tears.

"Okay," he continued. "Yer with us now. Yer a part of our team."

"Cletus might be bleeding on the floor," she just had to say.

"Let's get a little closer and then I'll go have a look," James said.

I'd had enough of being carried and so I did my best at dog-trotting to the entrance. Plus, I was beginning to think that my ankle just might be more bruised than sprained; although it still throbbed. Suddenly, James halted us.

"The Plymouth's parked, but I don't see Derrick," he whispered. "You two wait here and I'll check the car."

Me and Pepper watched as James slinked up to the car.

James peeked inside and froze as he looked into the back seat.

"Ah oh," I murmured.

James stumbled back, tripped on something and fell. He quickly looked back at the mine and then around toward us. He crawled back to the Plymouth and peeked inside again.

"Something's wrong," I said to Pepper. "I better go see if I can help. You stay here."

"I'm coming with."

I just nodded. I didn't have the energy to argue.

"What is it?" I whispered to James. He looked at me and pointed inside. I looked into the back seat. Cletus was lying motionless, blood everywhere.

"Holy Cow-pies, Nelson," I whispered. "Is he dead?"

Pepper backed away, tears immediately welling in her eyes. James opened the door and tried to feel for a pulse. When Cletus let out a deep moan, all three of us about jumped out of our skins.

"He's alive!" James whispered. "Cletus, help us get you outta here."

A blank stare showed that Cletus didn't recognize us.

"Come on, Cleets! We're trying to help you," I said.

We grabbed his arm and started pulling, but he was a 300-pound load. Finally, he dug deep and started helping. Unfortunately, he didn't make it out of the car on his feet, landing on the ground, collapsed in a huge heap. He had been shot in at least two places. His shoulder was oozing blood, but his stomach was a mess. I ripped away a heavy piece of cloth from Cletus' ragged jacket.

"Pepper, I need you to hold this on his stomach. Keep pressure, but not too hard or he might yelp."

"We need to hide you," I said to Cletus as the three of us tried to get him standing. "You can stay with Pepper behind that clump of trees."

He nodded and we all worked together to find a safe spot against a tree.

"Where's Derrick?" James asked Cletus. He just shook his head.

"Don't like blood," Cletus groaned.

"Pepper will take care of you," I assured.

"We'll be back," James said, looking directly at his little sister.

We headed out, James signaling that we first go toward the Plymouth.

I was baffled as he grabbed the keys from the ignition, then opened the trunk. He lugged out the spare tire, then shut the trunk and replaced the keys. Just in time, because I now saw a light on the walls of the mine.

"Here he comes," I whispered. We shoved the tire under the car and made it to the trees when Derrick came hurrying out of the mine. He stood at the gaping hole in the mountain and shined his light around in frantic waves, searching the trees and rocks that were littered around the entrance. We hunkered lower and made sure fir branches covered our faces. Derrick dashed back into the mine, but just for a few seconds. When he came back out, he started running down the road, probably looking to see if we were coming.

"Look at him," I whispered. "He doesn't know what to do."

Sure enough, Derrick returned to the mine and disappeared inside.

"We can't go in the main entrance," James whispered, "so we'll need to skirt around to the little vent."

"What's with the tire?" I asked.

"We're gonna need it," he said. "Let's go."

After recovering the tire from under the car, we headed toward the side vent. A spare tire isn't something two kids can carry, so James rolled it as best as he could. As if I didn't already have enough trouble walking, the ground was rocky and blocked with dead trees and roots. I kept looking back for Derrick. When he'd run out of the mine, we'd stop and watch.

"He looks frustrated that we've not shown up," I whispered. "Uh oh."

Derrick stopped at the car. Even from a hundred yards away, we could see by his movements that he was completely confused that Cletus was gone.

"Cleets?" Derrick said, but didn't yell. "Where are ya, Cuz?"

"If he finds him and Pepper . . ." I didn't finish saying the obvious.

Derrick hurried down the road. That seemed the logical place for Cletus to escape. James tugged my sleeve and we took off as fast as we could. Once we were out of view of the entrance, we made good time. Well, James made good time. I was losing energy trying to climb the side of the mountain. He dropped the tire a few times and helped me.

"Get that thing to the vent and wait for me," I said. "I'll get there."

"Nope, we're together on this one, Calvin Poag," he grunted while getting me and the tire up the hill.

Fifteen minutes later, we were inside the pitch black tube. Then a match suddenly lit up the tiny tunnel.

"Look what was laying on the car seat," James said, holding up a book of matches. He was grinning and I couldn't help but punch his shoulder. We'd light one every twenty feet of so, but at that rate we were going to run out fast.

"We gotta find something to burn," I whispered.

"I know," James agreed.

From there it was mostly downhill and the tire carried its own weight. We just had to keep it under control. Near where the vent tube met the main shaft was a small wide spot with some tools and machines.

"Maybe we can find something here," I suggested, and started looking around. I grabbed a huge screwdriver and tried scraping axle grease from the wheel of an old ore cart. We were going through matches fast.

"Look." I held up a mangled grease gun. I worked the lever and a tiny bit of thick, green paste oozed out. I tore off a bit of my hospital gown and wrapped the handle of the screwdriver. James pumped out a little more grease, we smeared the cloth, and lit it. Poof. A smoky flame gave us plenty of light and we took off for the water.

I think James was surprised when I just shoved the tire in and started swimming. Any fears I had about water monsters had shrunk next to being caught by Derrick. All I wanted to do was get that chest and get out of there. But, whatever was in the water was stinging all my cuts and scrapes.

"This water is burning!"

"Yeah, my burns are burning," James agreed. "We're gonna have to work fast, Cal. If we have to douse this torch, we might never get it going again." The thought of being stuck down here without any light sent my imagination into high gear. I looked at the torch. It was hissing and spitting, but still burning.

I kept wondering what Derrick was up to. If he'd found Cletus, he'd find Pepper and know that we were here. Who knew what would happen then. The thought made me shiver . . . even more than the cold water.

We reached the shore just in time because I felt like I was going to come unglued. We crawled out and James immediately pried the back off the grease gun and started digging inside for more of the flammable goo. What he found would add maybe another fifteen minutes. I jammed the torch into a crack and we went to work.

The plan was to lift the chest with a rope, place it on the tire, and float it through the water. The chest was so heavy, but we did manage to lift it. One problem . . . we couldn't get the rope to slide on the pipe. I held it while James scrambled out over the water and got things moving. We then maneuvered the chest directly over the tire and carefully let it down.

"It's going to flip over," I pointed out.

"No, we'll tie it on and it'll float, I think," James said as we laced the rope through the tire rim and the chest's handles.

"He knows where you live," I blurted. "How're you going

to hide this?"

"We'll figure something. He's not gettin' these coins, I am."

"We could hide it in the cheese caves," I suggested halfheartedly. In the back of my mind, I was still thinking of all the horrible ways this could end.

"Well, let's go swimming," he said and again we shoved the tire and chest out into the black water. The tire instantly wobbled and rolled, but it didn't sink.

"It's holding," James said.

It seemed like a miracle . . .

Chapter 20

ALL FOR ME, NONE FOR YOU

I held the torch as we quietly paddled through the water with our feet, pushing the chest on the tire. We got around the first bend in the shaft and the second . . . and there was Derrick, standing on the shore shining his light at us.

"That's ingenious, boys. Great idea. It's like we're partners or something." He grinned and even clapped.

We stopped dead in the water, about a hundred feet from the shore.

"Oh, don't stop," he said. "You're doin' great. Just paddle right on up here and we can call it a night." We couldn't see him because his light was in our eyes, but we started to back up.

BANG! His gun went off and the bullet kicked up the water right next to me. We both instantly ducked down behind the tire and kicked hard, in reverse. BANG! Derrick fired again. This time he hit the tire and it started to hiss.

"Uh oh, did you boys get a flat? Better get it over here so we can fix it."

But we were already around the bend in the shaft. We shifted around so we could kick from behind.

"Guys, come on!" Derrick suddenly sounded disappointed and tired of this whole ordeal. He then snorted out a laugh and yell. "I can do this all night, ya know!"

"Kick, Cal," James whispered.

"Wadda think I'm doing?" I whispered back.

Even so, I couldn't keep up with James and I was running out of gas, fast. Weird, though, my ankle didn't hurt as much . . . the rest of me still did.

"What are we gonna do now?" I asked.

"Get back to the other side and . . . I guess we hide this chest again."

Derrick had quit yelling, so I figured he was on his way back to the entrance, and then around to meet us.

"Bet he found Pepper and scared our plan outta her," I said. Probably tied her to a tree, I thought, but didn't say that part out loud.

At the shore, the torch was just barely sputtering. James frantically scraped the sides of the grease gun tube and rubbed what he found on the torch as I got the chest untied and our rope coiled. What were we going to do with it?

"We gotta hide this thing so we can run," I said.

James stopped for just a second.

"The control room," he blurted. "Yer right, we'll hide it and come back later . . . our original plan."

We each grabbed a handle and started hauling.

* * *

The control room was exactly that. It's where the head miners ran everything. Lots of wires ran into the room because all the electrical things were controlled from there. I figured the miners watched the steam pressure in there too because there were some huge pipes and valves.

The coolest part was the electrical panels with switches and glass gauges. The long desk had more gauges and big door-knob size dials. It reminded me of a space ship in a movie; James said it looked more like the control room on a ship. Naturally, we'd claimed it as our main hideout. The problem . . . it was on the upper shaft.

* * *

We stopped trying to be quiet. We stumbled and fell and banged into things as we hurried toward Shaft #3. We knew it'd take Derrick a while to get back around to the entrance and then down to us.

"What about Pepper?" I asked, as we lugged the heavy chest toward where we hoped we could escape.

"I dunno, Cal. He's probably got her wadded up in the trunk with Cletus." That looked very crowded in my mind's view.

"Let's trade him, like we were going to do with Cletus," I suggested.

"What? This for her?" James asked and banged the chest.

"No, me for her," I said sarcastically. "Yes, *this* for her!"

James didn't say anything for a few seconds. The fact that he seemed to be weighing the options made me mad. I stopped trotting and dropped my end of the chest. I was out of breath anyway.

"Come on," he said, angry that we had stopped.

"No!"

I just stood there looking at him.

"This is serious biz, Cal. Pick up your end and let's get going!"

"Give me my half of the coins and I'll trade it for Pepper."

"Your half? You didn't even wanna help me two hours ago," he snarled.

"Well, here I am. Carrying *my* half. So now I want it."

"This is ridiculous," he snapped and shoved me to the ground. He grabbed the chest and started dragging it along the floor of the mine. It made a loud scraping sound that I was sure Derrick would hear if he was back in the mine.

"That creep's gonna get the whole thing," James continued. "And then kill us and Pepper if you don't help me!"

He was right. At least we had what Derrick desperately wanted, so we had something to bargain with. I didn't say anything. I just got back to my feet, grabbed my half, and we got going again. We didn't talk, we just worked.

I was trying to calculate how long it would take Derrick to go around the mountain while we were going through it. The math wasn't working. We weren't going to get to the control room in time. And, we were moving back toward Derrick.

"We're not going to make it," I huffed out. "He's probably already inside the mine." We stopped for a second, James thinking about what I'd said.

"Shaft #3," he said.

I groaned. "Then what?"

"Well, I guess we're back down at the bottom again," he said.

Now we were going around in circles. Still, I decided not to argue or try to come up with a better plan, so I grabbed my handle and we took off again.

Shaft #3 was about halfway between us and the control room. It wasn't going to be easy getting this heavy chest down through all that tangle of junk.

"Hear that?" I whispered. "He's in the main shaft."

"He doesn't care about being quiet either," James said. We were almost out of breath when we turned the corner and started down the spur that led to Shaft #3.

"Sorry I shoved you," James said once we were out of sight of the main shaft. He mostly looked at the ground. Sorry is not a word James is used to saying. I figured it took everything in him to get it out. I gave him a little shoulder punch.

"I'm just thinking about Pepper," I said.

"Me too, but I'm also thinking about my mom."

Okay, I thought. "We can figure this out, James." I saw his face brighten. He nodded, yes.

"Come on," he whispered.

Chapter 21

SHOWDOWN IN THE SHAFT

Because the short spur had a number of twists and turns, we figured Derrick probably wouldn't see the light from our torch. But, he'd definitely smell the smoke.

When we reached the giant hole to the shaft, we dug into the grease gun one more time, hoping there'd be a miracle glob we'd missed. There was some in the end tube and we again smeared the handle of the screwdriver and it brightened. I quickly tied the rope to one of the chest's handles and started lowering it down through the tangle of junk. The rope would burn our hands if we let it go too fast, so we needed to take our time. Plus, it kept hanging up on things, so we had to continually lift and shift.

We heard a sharp yelp and stopped.

"He's got Pepper," I whispered. I could see that James was torn about what to do.

"We're almost there," he muttered.

The light from our tiny torch didn't really reach the bottom of the shaft, but we felt the chest finally land and we let go of the rope.

"You first," I whispered.

"Good call," he answered. "That way I don't step on your head when you get stuck."

I gave him a serious look.

"I'm not getting stuck, James."

He quickly grabbed the first pipe and swung out and dropped down to the nearest massive beam. He balanced and then crab-walked out to the middle where he jumped down to the next beam.

I heard another yelp and looked back down the spur.

They were getting close.

I grabbed the first pipe and did my best version of what I'd seen James do. If he looked like a smooth acrobatic spider monkey, I'm sure I looked like an overfed koala bear.

Already halfway down, James accidentally dropped the screwdriver torch and it bounced off beams and hit the floor. It amazed me that it didn't go out, but now the shaft was a lot darker.

I dropped down to the next big beam and did a crabwalk. Actually, it was more like a scoot-shuffle, but it worked. James was getting further and further down the shaft, so I was losing track of his steps and route. It didn't help that the tiny torch was clear down on the floor and not giving much light.

I looked down, sucked in my breath, and kept moving. This time, though, I more jumped and sprang than inched from beam to beam . . . my ankle held. Grabbing pipes and bolts, I was making progress when I heard Derrick skid to a stop at the top of the shaft. I looked up.

"You two, you think you can get away? Look who I got with me," he shouted, sounding all joyful while shoving a terrified Pepper out near the edge. She screamed through a handkerchief gag. I stopped. Derrick had a flashlight and its beam was darting off the walls and ceiling while he struggled to hold onto Pepper. She was making it very hard with all her wiggling around.

"Hey," I shouted.

"You hurt her and you get none of this!" James shouted back up the shaft.

"I'm gettin' all of it, stupid punks," Derrick yelled. "You got no idea who you're dealing with. I'm holdin' the best cards here." He scared Pepper again by leaning her out over the lip of the shaft, then yanked her back and I heard a scuffle break out.

Suddenly, Pepper jumped off the edge and grabbed the first pipe, like they were the monkey bars at school. She landed on a beam, steadied herself, and started to crabwalk the narrow length of wood. But, right behind her, Derrick jumped on the first beam with a hard landing. Obviously, it'd been a while since he had played on the monkey bars. He was off-balance and wobbly.

"AHHH!" he yelled when he landed. He got up and snarled at Pepper. "You little puke!" He moved as fast as he could across the beam and caught up with her.

"Push him," James shouted up at her. Derrick had a hold of her hospital gown but she squirmed free and gave him a hard shove. He yelled and cursed as he again lost balance. The tangle of junk below saved him from falling all the way to the bottom. The trouble . . . now he was below Pepper.

If he kills himself, this nightmare is over, I thought. I even thought about praying for that to happen. But for some reason, praying for someone to get killed didn't feel right. I knew for sure that Gram or Gramps would frown on that idea. So I dropped it and instead went back to getting away.

Suddenly, a sharp "BANG" made my ears ring, followed by that zing sound bullets make when they ricochet off something. It was deafening in the shaft. I was looking down when he fired and saw James dodge to the side. I looked up and Pepper was cowering against the wall. Derrick was frantically pulling the trigger of his pistol, but all he got was "click, click, click."

"He's out of bullets," James cheered.

"Come on, Pepper," I yelled up at her. She was on one side of the shaft and Derrick was stuck on the other. In no time Pepper had made it down another ten feet while Derrick was still trying to find good footing and handholds. Dust was raining down on me and James from all the scrambling above us and it got in my eyes and I started sneezing. Then a handful of bullets showered down on us. Derrick had tried to reload, but dropped them. A couple of the bullets landed on the beam near me and I kicked them down to James, who quickly gathered them up.

"You punks," Derrick hollered. "That's my chest!"

James had found a few chunks of wood down there and rescued our tiny torch. I was trying to keep one eye on Pepper working her way down and the other on my own progress. Without bullets, Derrick forgot about his gun and went back to chasing.

"Hurry, Pepper," James yelled.

Derrick was grunting and snarling as he stepped, swayed, grabbed things, and crab-walked across beams. I glanced up and saw him make a bold move. He jumped down to a lower beam and kicked at Pepper. He hit her in the shoulder and she slammed into the stone wall. He set his flashlight on the beam, dropped down, and grabbed her. He had his hands full, trying to hold Pepper and not fall to his death. And she was not making it easy. This was all happening about ten feet above me.

I stopped going down and reached for a pipe, heaving myself back on the beam above me. I scrambled to the next beam and rolled up and sat on it.

"You're mine, Pepper," Derrick barked, but she had other ideas.

"Hold on," James yelled, and started climbing back up the ladder.

"Don't worry, she's not goin' nowhere," Derrick shouted back at him, and laughed.

I was much closer. They were on the beam above me. I tried to reach some huge bolts in the wall, but missed and wobbled wildly when I landed. But that was my only option. I stepped back, ran toward the wall, and jumped again.

As my hand latched onto the bottom bolt, I pulled with everything I had to grab the next bolt. Three more and I was on the beam. Derrick whipped around and glared at me with crazed eyes. He had Pepper locked in one arm and his other hand was grasping some tattered wires that were attached to the wall.

"Come on, ya little twerp," he snarled at me, but Pepper was keeping him busy. He kept trying to lift her off the beam to keep her from wiggling so much, but she'd kick him or the wall, pushing both of them off balance.

"Trade you," I said. "Me for her."

"What? Are you kiddin'?" He gave her a shake. "You think I'd trade her for you? Forget it, Chump."

He looked toward the bottom of the shaft.

"I'll trade with you, James," Derrick yelled. "Your sister for the chest."

"I'm not kidding," I said. "Let her go."

"I don't want any of you," he said to me. "You ain't worth nothin'. . . . I want my chest and you all can go home."

"Right," James yelled up. "We all just go home and pretend none of this ever happened."

"I can live with that," Derrick yelled back.

"How about a split?" James yelled back up. Derrick looked down at him and that's when I rushed them. I had no plan other than freeing Pepper. What happened next is kind of a blur. Pepper fell and landed on the beam below. Derrick and I smashed into the wall and he hit his head and went kind of limp, slumping down to a crouched position. His flashlight rolled off the beam and crashed through the junk that crisscrossed the shaft, shattering on the floor below. Shaft #3 again turned dim, our flickering torch providing the only light. I quickly latched onto the wires that Derrick had been holding and stayed on the beam. Below us, Pepper was hurt.

"Come on, Pepps," James said. "See that pipe? The one right over your head on the wall. Grab it!" She got ahold of it and overhanded to the bolts I'd used the first time I was down there. Derrick was coming around. His head was bleeding and he looked a bit confused.

"You win that round," he muttered, "but I ain't done."

When I grabbed the first bolt to start moving down

again, I noticed how some of the rocks on the wall were loose.

"Look out, James!" I yelled and heaved a baseball-size rock at Derrick. It hit him in the hand and he screamed out. My thoughts went back to Derrick falling and killing himself. I decided not to think too much about it and started working rocks free from the wall and lining them up in a row on the beam.

Between rocks hitting him and hiding from getting hit, Derrick slowed down enough to allow Pepper to move faster. I just had to be careful that I didn't hit her. I had him pinned under a big beam so Pepper could make the jump to the platform and start down the ladder. When she reached the bottom, James rushed her out of sight and I went full auto with my rocks. He had to curl up. One hit his shoulder. Another smashed him in the head. While I was digging out some more rocks, he made a jump for it. He was now below me and I showered more rocks down on him. Trying to dodge and escape with someone bombing you with rocks was not easy and he found himself stranded on a log that didn't go anywhere. His only choice was a six-foot jump to try and grab some bolts on the wall. I stuffed a few rocks in my gown pockets and started climbing down. Every time Derrick even thought about making a lunge, I threw him my best fastball. While I had him dodging rocks, I kept working my way down through the tangled mess, again reaching the same level as Derrick.

"When I get hold of you, Cal, I'm gonna tear you to pieces!" I just glanced at him and kept going down.

I reached the steam pipe and grabbed it and started to hand-over-hand my way to where the platform had joined the wall. This time, I knew to land on the right side and sprung through the open shaft. I heard growls and grunts up above me. Then a terrible scream as Derrick flew past me and hit the platform, his leg smashing right through the rotten wood. He was jammed and just hung there . . .

unconscious . . . a full-sized Raggedy Andy doll.

"Wow," James gasped.

I then jumped and landed on the good side. I was only six feet from Derrick and needed to get away as fast as I could. If he woke up, he might be able to grab me. When I finally made it down to the floor, my legs turned to rubber and I collapsed. Pepper ran up and grabbed me, helping me down the shaft and away from Derrick.

James, though, stood and stared up at Derrick. He grabbed the rope and started up the ladder.

"What are you doing?" I whispered, not wanting to risk waking Derrick.

"You'll see," he whispered back. When he could reach Derrick's dangling arms, he tied them together and then threw the rope over the nearest beam. He climbed down and started to pull it up. The motion woke Derrick and he screamed out in pain, but James gave the rope a strong tug.

"Be careful," I shouted. "You might kill him!"

"Not yer worst idea," James growled. He gave the rope another tug.

I looked up at Derrick.

"I don't think he's going anywhere, James. Let's get outta here and call the Sheriff."

"Yer done for, Derrick Carter," James said in a menacing voice. He hesitated, then let me tie off the rope to a rusty winch machine. James thumbed the rope to see if it was tight. It gave off a low "thung" sound.

"You better not leave me," Derrick shouted.

James grabbed one handle of the chest and I grabbed the other.

"Wait," Derrick screamed.

We'd lugged that chest about ten feet when James stopped. He hurried back and grabbed the best burning chunk of wood and stomped out the rest.

"No, come on, James," Derrick yelled. Suddenly all the

anger and confidence left Derrick's voice and what was left
was terror.

Chapter 22

ONE CROWDED CARLOAD

You've probably figured out that we had to drag that chest of coins back up the steep tunnel. Derrick screamed and hollered for us to come back. One minute he'd be threatening us with his deadly wrath and the next he'd be trying to bargain. James thought it was funny.

Pepper said the last time she had seen Cletus, he was curled up in a ball and crying out in pain, shaking like he was hooked to an electrical cord. She told us that when Derrick discovered them, he was going to shoot Cletus again but she'd thrown herself on top of the big man. Well, Derrick thought that was hilarious, and because he was in a big hurry, just scooped her up and kicked Cletus in the side.

Cletus was unconscious when we found him and had lost a lot of blood. Somehow, we got him into the back seat of the Plymouth where he collapsed into a giant bloody hulk. Pepper climbed in, wrapped Cletus in a stinky blanket she found on the floor, then sat with her arm around him.

We headed home, the front seat as crowded as the back with me driving, James at shotgun, and the treasure chest stuffed in between.

Having reopened the chest, James was fiddling with the coins, trying to count and calculate our new fortune.

"There's got to be hundreds of them," he murmured. "Look at this . . . 1851 . . . that's gotta be worth something."

He tried to show it to me, but I was more interested in what was behind us.

"What kind of knot did you use?" I asked.

"What do you mean?"

"On Derrick," I clarified with a touch of irritation.

"How should I know? A big one."

"A big one? I hope it was a good, big one."

"If I could have found more rope, I'd have wrapped him up like a mummy," James laughed and looked back at Pepper.

"I don't get why you care about that big slug," he said.

"Cuz he's hurt, James."

"Pepper, he stuffed you in a trunk and took you out to Carmelita's."

"He told me some stuff after you guys left. I feel bad for him."

"What stuff?"

"Stuff that Carmelita and her boys did to him. They've been robbing people's houses and stealing cars and stuff like that. Carmelita and Derrick both make Cletus do a lot of bad things."

"Like stealing coins," I interjected.

"Shut up Cal," James said softly, closing his eyes. "Stop at the cheese caves before we do anything else. We can hide them there.

In about a mile, both James and Pepper were asleep. Cletus just looked dead.

Chapter 23

SWIMMING IN A POT OF HOT WATER

The next few months were a whirlwind—questions, commotion, and the trial. Most of the time, I felt like I was swimming in a pot of my own hot water.

After hiding the treasure, we had taken Cletus straight to the hospital. The police arrived and we told them where they could find Derrick.

The doctors made Pepper and I stay at the hospital a couple of days for observation. It was nice having a clean hospital gown.

It was a good thing those Carters were in jail for kidnapping; it helped take some of the spotlight off me. Gram especially was glad I was okay, and being hurt helped some too. Uncle Neal, though, would sneak into my room when Gram was not around and start grilling me about what a bad boy I was and how I was going to give my Gram a heart attack with all my shenanigans.

Remember Doctor Floyd Carter? He stepped into my hospital room, his arm in a sling and head bandaged. My guess is that he'd been beaten up by Derrick for helping us to escape. He was glad we had survived.

I thanked him for the Chevy.

"Quite an ordeal," he said, keeping one eye on the door. "You've probably guessed that I try not to associate with that side of my family if I can help it. Carmelita is a very bad seed."

He smiled at me when he left, but I thought he looked kind of sad.

* * *

James was beaming when he came to visit.

"Derrick's in the slammer for a long time," he told me. "And not just for kidnapping us. He's in deep water about a bunch of mysterious things that've been happening on both sides of The Gorge . . . Oregon and Washington."

James pulled out two coins—one silver, one gold.

"There's a bunch of gold ones in that chest."

"I think we need to turn this in," I blurted out.

"What?" he almost shouted. He shushed himself and gave me a stern look. "Remember my mom? We need this, Cal."

"Have you told her?"

"Not yet," he said. "When things get a little quieter . . ."

"What if someone finds out? What if Derrick spills the beans? Everyone might think we're the ones who stole it. And even if we did say that we took them from Derrick, it'd still be a tangle of string to try and untie. We could end up in jail . . . in the same cell with Derrick!"

"Settle down, Cal. That's not gonna happen. I have a plan."

Here we go, I thought.

"Cal, don't you find it odd that no one has mentioned the chest of coins? Derrick doesn't want his momma to know that he's been doing side deals."

Okay, that's good, I guessed.

"This trial won't be about a treasure chest," James continued. "It's about them kidnapping us. We stick to the true story. Cletus kidnapped Pepper, we accidentally blew up their house when we were trying to rescue her, and then they kidnapped all of us . . . took us up river to probably sell us into slavery or something."

Judging by the way James looked at me, I am certain he expected me to applaud his brilliance.

"Only thing, James, why did they keep coming after us every time we escaped?"

"Simple, they had to keep chasing us because we could identify them as kidnappers. The last time we got away, we tried to hide in the mine with Derrick hot on our trail. But we trapped him before he killed us. We don't know why he shot Cletus, but he did."

Before I could come up with another reason why this all could backfire, the nurse came into the room. We immediately changed the subject.

"Have you seen Pepper?" I asked.

"She's doing great," James said. "I think she's hoping you'll come see her."

"Ohhh," I mumbled.

Chapter 24

THE WHOLE TRUTH

Although I was a tangle of nerves, James seemed excited that he would be center stage in the trial of the century. He reminded me and Pepper of our agreed-upon plan for us to tell the jury exactly what had happened, minus the chest of coins.

The trial took place at the Federal Courthouse up in Yakima, but that didn't keep most of Mud Lake from attending. I sat with Gram and Uncle Neal. Right next to us was James, Pepper, and Mrs. Nelson. We were directly behind the prosecuting attorney, but had a direct view of the jury. To our right—on the other side of the room—sat the Carter bunch. Dressed in orange prison outfits, they were crowded around a table with their lawyer, looking like a mob of trolls sitting down for a meal. The sheriffs in the room stood right behind them . . . just in case.

Derrick and Carmelita sat in the middle of the gang, with Cletus sitting to the side of the table in a wheelchair. He had been in a coma for nearly a month and had just been released from the hospital.

As luck would have it, I was the first witness called to the stand. My legs felt like mush.

A man had me put my left hand on the Bible and raise my right arm.

"Do you swear to tell the truth, the whole truth, and nothing but the truth . . . so help you God?"

"I do."

My mind suddenly felt like ping-pong balls were flying in a thousand directions. The truth . . . all of it . . . so help me God?

All I remember after that was looking at Gram when their lawyer quizzed me about why we were at the mine?

I crumbled.

"We were exploring when we saw Derrick and Cletus burying a treasure chest full of coins . . ."

There was more, of course, but not before the courtroom nearly had to be cleared. Carmelita shoved Derrick, then stood and pounded him on the side of his head, the sheriffs trying to restrain her. As for what she was shouting, I'm not sure I can repeat any of that stuff . . . a couple of words I had never even heard.

After the scuffle, I looked over at James, who was staring directly into my eyes. He then lowered his head into the cups of his hands.

The rest of the trial, James would hardly look at me. When he did, his eyes shot darts that probably could leave welts. Of course, he too now told the real story.

Gram said that I had done the right thing to give up the chest of coins, but I was devastated. Yes, I had told the truth, but I had messed up his plans to save his mom.

* * *

The Carters—every one of them—were found guilty. Thanks to a plea by Pepper, Cletus would only go to jail for a couple of years. Derrick received the longest sentence of the group and still had to face future trials for other bad deeds, including stealing that chest of coins.

After I spilled the beans and the police recovered the chest from our hiding spot, they also found the original owner, Mr. Vickers. Turns out Derrick had found out that Mr. Vickers had a collection of valuable coins. He drove over to Portland, broke into the house, and blew open the safe with dynamite.

* * *

Several days after the trial ended, Gram invited James, Pepper, and their mom over to the house for an "important meeting" with Mr. Vickers. Pepper sat next to me on the couch . . . maybe a bit too close. James, standing at the other side of the living room, pretended to be uninterested.

"James," said Mr. Vickers, "why don't you have a seat next to your sister. We have something to discuss."

Mr. Vickers started by calling me and James a couple of scallywags.

"You both remind me of me when I was your age," he added with a smile.

He had been raised in Portugal by an uncle who loved grubbing around in ancient forts and diving to old ship wrecks.

"So, the fact that you boys were in a mine, chasing treasure, swimming across inky water of unknown depth, runnin' down those Carters, and rescuing Pepper. I'll tell you this, by gum, I wish I was runnin' in your gang!"

He handed us three large books.

"People need to know their deeds are valued. And I value yours," he said. "Open them."

Our eyes about popped out of our heads. Tucked in little plastic pockets were two pages of old silver coins, twenty-four in all.

"I also have something even more special for you three," he said in a low and mysterious voice. When he opened another book, I heard Gram and Mrs. Nelson suck in some air.

"Holy cow," Uncle Neal muttered.

"Gold doubloons," said Mr. Vickers. "Two for each of you . . . each nearly five centuries old."

"I've had these coins since I was your age, nearly sixty years. Be wise with them and they'll provide a good portion of your future."

Mr. Vickers turned to look at Mrs. Nelson.

"I understand that the kids tried to take these coins with you in mind," he said. "And, after your husband's death, you have suddenly found yourself in a difficult predicament."

He then provided documents to Mrs. Nelson that would pay off all of the family's overdue bills and the mortgage to her house. He even handed a check to Gram to help with some of her bills. As you can imagine, Mr. Vickers had the entire house in tears . . . even James had leaky eyes.

At dinner that evening, Mr. Vickers told some great stories about exploring sunken ships and wondered if we might like to learn how to scuba dive.

"I know where there's an old barge sunk on the river," he said. "It just might have some interesting cargo."

"Wow," James blurted, his eyes wide open. "I'm in!"

I just nodded my head, instantly picturing myself stuck underwater with a herd of sea monsters.

James punched me on the shoulder . . . he knew what I was thinking.

THE END

NEXT IN THE SERIES – 2019

Between a Rock and a Hard Place
A Calvin Poag Adventure, Vol. 3

Cameron Ventura, Hidden Shelf Publishing House

After his Gram passes away, Cal's life is turned upside down (again) when Uncle Neal ships him off to the western coast of British Columbia. Leaving Mud Lake—and best friend James—is difficult, but things start to look up when he meets Adi, a girl with a Honda 90 motorbike, knowledge of a private island, and a penchant for adventure. Unfortunately, Cal's new friend is tangled up with some rather shady characters, pulling both of them into a heap of intrigue and danger. So, when things spin out of control, Adi and Cal's survival suddenly includes life-and-death decisions as they find themselves *Between A Rock and a Hard Place*!

COLLECT THE ENTIRE SERIES

Do or Die Time
A Calvin Poag Adventure, Vol. 1

Cameron Ventura & Dennis Mansfield,
Hidden Shelf Publishing House, 2017

When Cal and James discover something terrible in the woods, their youthful curiosity unexpectedly leads them on a path that soon threatens their very survival . . . a fast-paced adventure requiring physical prowess, mental toughness, and unwavering trust. Best friends caught in the most perilous situation of their lives, welcome to *Do or Die Time*!

On sale now at Amazon.com and wherever fine books are sold . . .

ABOUT THE AUTHOR
Cameron Ventura

Back when he was a freshman in high school, Cameron Ventura inherited his grandfather's photography equipment. Four decades later, he is an established filmmaker, writer, photographer, and musician—a long and creative path of telling visual stories.

Cameron and his wife, Linda, live on a small farm in Idaho. Follow him at www. CameronVentura.com

Acknowledgements

First off, thanks to my wife, Linda, for her support and willingness to read all my prose—*worts 'n all*. I'd like to thank Dennis Mansfield for his always generous insight and encouragement. Charles (Chuck) Mangun for helping with pacing and climbing techniques, and for inviting me to write-around-the-campfire in the back country of Idaho. Scott Ziemer, my faithful, insightful, and always willing literary chum. My editors, Kathy Gaudry and Bob Gaines. You both make it easy to change, grow, and hopefully improve. Paula and Christy and the Lowell Scott gang, your critiques and insight made *It's Now or Never* better. My cover models— Zach, Bailey, Hadyn—guys, you brought it. Thanks McDonald family, for your tremendous support throughout this long process. Steve Van Atta for the guidance and direction. And of course, my friend and savior, Jesus, for letting me share fun places and experiences through my writing.